Sapphire Dragon

TERRY BOLRYDER

Copyright © 2016 Terry Bolryder

All rights reserved.

ISBN: 1537111264
ISBN-13: 978-1537111261

DEDICATION

For Mattie

CONTENTS

Acknowledgments	i
Prologue	1
Chapter One	5
Chapter Two	21
Chapter Three	34
Chapter Four	46
Chapter Five	57
Chapter Six	76
Chapter Seven	92
Chapter Eight	102
Chapter Nine	115
Chapter Ten	126
Chapter Eleven	142
Chapter Twelve	153
Chapter Thirteen	167
Chapter Fourteen	183
Chapter Fifteen	193
Chapter Sixteen	210

Chapter Seventeen	221
Chapter Eighteen	233
Epilogue	247

ACKNOWLEDGMENTS

Many thanks to my wonderful husband, my cute pets, my loving family, and my trusty keyboard. And huge thanks to the readers to make it all worth it!

PROLOGUE

Lucien beat his sapphire wings hard as he surveyed the devastation beneath him, as if by rising in the air, he could somehow go far enough away to not see what he was witnessing.

When he'd made his daily journey to fly over his favorite village, he could never have expected this.

Burned fields, the smell of singed crops, singed houses, singed lives in the air. His dragon let out a cry as his wings carried him higher over his beloved town.

Not that he'd ever been a part of it. Not that he'd ever been one of them as a human.

But it had been his hope for humanity. There were people he knew there, people he had healed, sneaking in while in human form. People who had showed him kindness. People whose crops he had watered while hiding behind clouds in the bright-blue sky.

And now there was nothing. Desolation. Pain. Sorrow.

He landed with a thud and surveyed the blackened landscapes. Moldering skeletons of burned-down shacks, charred shapes on the burned ground.

Tears bit his eyes as he took human form to make his way around the village, checking for survivors.

But he already knew.

There were none.

Part of his ability as a dragon was hearing people in pain, hearing thoughts more acutely so he knew where to heal them. Where they needed him. At this point, he was probably the only dragon who cared about humans.

But he'd met a few that changed everything for him.

And now, he realized, looking over the devastated landscape, they were gone.

Everything he'd done was for nothing. Everything he'd worked for.

He could still scent the strangers that had done this. The worst part was they were from a village not far from there. One where factions often had problems with the villagers here. But still, bloodshed? Fire?

The other dragons had tried to tell him it was pointless to intervene, but they hadn't heard what he did. They didn't know what he knew.

Humans could be good at times. The problem was, he realized bitterly, the bad humans would ruin it for everyone, so any interference was pointless.

Inside him, he felt his heart harden. What had once been a fluid energy ready to heal and soothe now felt icy and cold. He let out a long breath and saw ice needles form in the air before him.

He grinned and listened to the wind, gauging its direction. Then he let his wings grow, felt himself transition back into the giant blue dragon he was.

Sparkling, glistening wings, touched by ice. A long, graceful body and pointed head with bright-yellow eyes. Nothing like his eyes in human form.

He floated upward, beating the air around him, not caring who saw as he went higher, higher, trying to make out those who had done this. Were they back at the village?

The ground was still warm. It was at least a day's journey back to where they'd come from.

There was nothing he could do for Anna or anyone else he'd cared about.

But there was something he could do to make himself feel better. He soared through the clouds until he made out the band of robbers walking the road back to their village. Slightly singed, still carrying torches and weapons. And then he heard the most hideous thing of all. Laughter. They were celebrating.

They'd ended the lives of the few humans Luc cared about, wasting years of study, years of interference, and they were *laughing*.

He dove toward them, freezing the ice in his chest, ready to release killing breath.

CHAPTER 1

Modern Day

"What should we do?" Erin asked Zach as they both watched Lucien in his typical daily activity. "He's been like this for days."

Zach folded his arms and stared at the human version of the dragon he'd most admired back in his day.

Some had said Sapphire, or Lucien, was stupid because he'd been interested in helping humans while others had been more interested in pillaging and storing treasure.

But Zach had always thought it denoted a bit of inner strength—to go his own way—if nothing else.

Even if Zach had once thought humans weren't worth saving.

Now, though, with his arm around his mate, happily adjusting to his place in the world, he knew better. And that made him respect the other dragon even more.

The problem was at some point, Lucien had changed.

Where he had once been compassionate, sharing long nights arguing with Zach over the issues with humans, everything had turned upside down sometime before they had gone into their deep sleep.

The Sapphire Zach saw before him was nothing like the man he'd known.

Cold. Closed off. Still handsome, as all dragons were. Still tall and strong, with probably some of his considerable powers, even with the thick collar around his neck, ensuring he didn't take full dragon form.

But aside from his outer appearance—his blond hair, his astonishing eyes that contained every shade of blue, his large build—nothing else was the same.

"Luc, you have to get out," Zach said, kicking the

back of Luc's chair to get the other man's attention. Luc had taken to sitting in a large, wingback chair, facing the window. "The oracle sent you out here for me to help you, and I'm not going to just let you mope."

"It's not your choice, is it?" Luc said in a low voice.

"You need to get out and meet humans. It's not good for you to be alone."

"Humans suck," Luc muttered, not even looking at them.

"Hey," Erin protested.

Luc gave a shrug. "Sorry."

Zach and Erin shared a concerned glance, unsure what to do, as they heard a quiet mew and Bo walked between their legs and over to their house guest.

Erin was about to stop him, but Zach put out a hand for her to let him be, and they both watched as the little black kitten walked awkwardly over to sit in front of Luc and look up at him with curious yellow eyes.

Bo was an irresistible ball of fluff as far as Zach was concerned. No one could say no to him.

But as Bo put up a paw, and Luc made no response, Zach wondered what was really wrong with his friend if he could ignore such a cute kitten.

But Bo's power finally won out as Luc slowly patted his leg, signaling for the cat to hop up, which he did, purring.

Zach smiled as he felt the energy in the room soften slightly. He could see Luc's hand moving gently over the kitten's back, making it arch. Then over his face and ears. Bo rolled onto his side, marking Luc with his cheeks, and then curled up into a comfy ball.

Zach heard a sigh from Luc's direction. Then he had an idea. He walked forward, leaning on the windowsill and facing Luc, who paid him no attention. "Why don't we go to the shelter? Get you one of your own?"

Luc lifted Bo by the scruff. "One like this?"

"Yes," Zach said. "Put him down."

Luc did, gently, and Bo snuggled in again.

"He likes you," Erin said.

Luc shrugged, but as unaffected as he tried to be, Zach could tell the idea intrigued him. If he wasn't going out into the world and he insisted on staying alone, then perhaps it wouldn't be a bad idea to get him a furry companion. Maybe melt his icy heart a bit.

"I heard that," Luc muttered.

Zach just laughed. "I thought you weren't interested in reading minds."

Luc shrugged. "Human minds are easy to ignore. Dragon thoughts are like shouting."

"Maybe you're getting back some of your empathy and healing."

Luc didn't answer.

Even the feeling around Luc wasn't the same as before. Being around his friend had always been somewhat calming, healing, unless he flew into an icy rage. But that was always temporary.

Until now, where he seemed permanently chilled, at least inside.

"Stop thinking about me," Luc said. "I don't need your pity. I just need to be put back to sleep. If she'd just give back my powers, I'd go back on ice myself."

Zach shook his head. "If you'd just give the world a chance, you might not want to."

Luc went silent again, and Bo's purr was the loudest noise in the quiet room. "So you say I can find one of these? If I go to this so-called shelter?"

"Yes," Zach said. "Erin and I will go with you. If you're going to mope around, you might as well have something to warm you." He narrowed his eyes. "And Bo is mine."

Luc gently set the kitten down so it could toddle over to Zach and rub against his legs, weaving in and out of them.

Zach grinned and lifted Bo into his arms, pressing his cheek to his soft fur. "Well, let's go get you one. None will be as cool as mine, but—"

"Zach." Erin interrupted as Luc stood and stretched, looking apathetic about life as usual. "Not the time."

"Right," Zach said. "To the shelter."

* * *

Lucien still felt dead inside, as he had since he'd woken, as they walked to the shelter.

At first, there had been some small measure of excitement as he'd gotten used to technology. But that had quickly worn off when he realized, compared to dragon magic, nothing was that astounding.

He was still figuring out the whole internet thing but hadn't found much use in it.

Not that there was any point, since he was just waiting for the oracle to give up on him and put him back to sleep.

He'd tried to help humans before. Fought for it with other dragons. Been a bastion of compassion and aid.

And look where that had gotten him.

Frozen inside and out.

The shelter was a small building with a sign out front with a cat and a dog on it. Animals that weren't too different than when he'd been alive.

He'd never particularly liked animals, mainly because he hadn't been around a lot of them, but if Bo were any indication, they had a lot on people in the character department.

He felt a touch of nerves as he followed Erin and Zach up to the double doors that led into the building. There was a small but clean waiting room with a front desk behind a counter that separated a room of office workers from the main space where people could wait.

He sat on one of the hard benches as Zach and Erin spoke with the person at the front desk.

He had no interest in talking to any human and would wait until they were ready to present him with options for pets. At least something to hold might make his time here a little more bearable.

But just as he was sitting there, minding his own business, he felt a wave of pain shoot through him.

He bolted straight up, looking around the room. No one in visible distress.

But it had been a long time since he'd felt hurt strong enough to reach past the walls he'd erected around his heart.

He'd realized long ago that he could only take so much of it, and it didn't do much good in the end anyway.

But for some reason, this person's pain was reaching out to him.

Shuttering his expression, he stuck his hands in his pockets and walked up to the front desk to join Erin and Zach.

A soft-spoken, curvy woman with long, dark hair and soft-gray eyes that almost appeared purple when they caught the light gave him a gentle smile.

"Is this the adopter?" she asked Erin and Zach.

They nodded, wary. They needn't have been. Luc knew how to be polite. He wasn't a monster.

"I'm looking for a pet," he said. But he wasn't really thinking about that. Instead, he was wondering if this woman could be the one sending him pain. He no longer felt it at the moment, as she handed them paperwork and continued smiling and talking. But he braced himself, knowing it could happen again.

He looked at the other two women in the shelter—One on the phone, arguing with someone about a bill, another busy on the computer.

He felt another wave of pain as the woman speaking to them stood and came out to join them through a side door. A pleasant smile lit her face as she waved for them to follow.

"Let's go meet the animals," she said, turning to walk away with just the slightest limp.

He was ready this time and closed himself off to the pain so he wouldn't feel it anymore. Now that he knew where it was coming from, he didn't need to endure it.

He knew someone needed healing, but he also knew he couldn't do it.

What did baffle him was the easy way she spoke, how well she hid what she felt, how pleasant she remained as she walked them slowly down rows of cages of animals, explaining how each was special and who would make the proper owner.

She stopped and glanced over at him, waiting for his input, and he took the time to truly look her over.

She was short and rounded, with the type of figure that men and dragons in his day adored. Everything about her was soft, from her arms to her rounded shoulders to her curved stomach and hips. She was wearing a soft gray sweater that set off her eyes and made her look eminently huggable. Along with comfy black pants that probably made it easier to cope with whatever injury she was dealing with.

Watching her wince as she reached into a cage to

show them another option, he wanted his powers back. Now.

Whatever her pain was, he wanted to end it.

It was odd that this woman had made him feel that again.

He stepped past Erin and Zach, who were cooing over a possible kitten, and walked to the cages on the far side.

One particular cat sat in a cage with no one around him. He was hairless, with just a light coat of down on his white and pink body and huge, curious blue eyes and giant ears for his petite, graceful face and long body.

But even at a cursory glance, Luc knew something was wrong. The cat wasn't acting like the others.

"Tell me about this one," he said bluntly, stopping in front of the crate.

The girl who'd been helping them made her way over. "You could say please," she said.

He turned to her in shock, only to see she was teasing. "Oh."

"My name's Hallie. I met your friends, but since it's your pet we're picking out, I'll need to know more about you as well."

He shoved his hands in his pockets. "I like this one." He lied. It wasn't so much that he liked him as he felt something was off. He *pitied* him.

"Oh," she said, her face unable to cover a tinge of sadness as she reached out to touch the cage, letting the cat sniff her hand gingerly. "He's not adoptable."

"Why not?" Luc asked, peering in closer.

She let out a breath and opened the cage, letting the slender creature crawl into her arms. Immediately, it rolled onto its back and purred. "Sphinxes are different, aren't they?"

"Ugly," Zach said, and Erin smacked his arm.

"I think they're kind of interesting," Erin said.

Luc thought Hallie was kind of interesting. The way she made animals relax in bliss, like the purring cat in front of him.

For a second, he wanted to be the one relaxing in bliss in her arms. The thought nearly made him jump back it was so foreign.

He'd never had a thought like that about a human in all his life. Maybe an occasional shifter back in his day, but never a human.

He blinked at her and tried to tune in to what she was saying as she lifted one of the cat's legs, showing a grotesque bulge. She had a pert nose and full lips that pursed as she looked at it.

"He has cancer," she explained. "Unfortunately, an aggressive kind that doesn't respond well to treatment. In his case, we found out it had already spread and can't be removed through surgery." She sighed. "It's a rare reaction to immunizations. Unlucky little guy." She put him back in.

"So what will happen to him?" Zach asked, frowning.

"He's not in a lot of discomfort, so we'll keep trying to make his life good until he's in pain, and then we'll help him go."

"You mean kill him?" Luc asked, shocked.

"Yes," she said flatly.

Luc was confused. He couldn't imagine this angelic woman killing anybody.

She turned back to the cat with soft eyes. "We give them the best life we can, and then we let them go gently. It's the last gift we give."

Luc felt another wave of attraction toward Hallie. It wasn't just her cute face or pretty body. It was the spirit emanating from her. Caring and brave. Courageous even.

Ugh, he was getting involved with humans again. Maybe this had been a bad idea.

He turned to make a run for it, but something stopped him. Maybe it was the purr of the cat abruptly stopping as he stepped away.

Maybe it was the thought of not seeing that beautiful, gray-eyed lady again. But he couldn't just walk away.

And then he noticed a sign posted on the wall. *Volunteers needed.*

Hmm.

"So can he not be fostered?" Erin asked sadly. "Just to give him some place comfortable?"

"I don't know," Hallie said. "It's against policy simply because we need to be able to treat him. As much as we can."

Luc walked over to the cat, and it started purring again. He raised an eyebrow and lifted his hand to stroke along its head, and its eyes closed in relief.

Perhaps he still had a little of his power after all. He examined the lump on its leg. Perhaps with time…

"What does it mean, volunteer?" he asked, pointing at the sign.

Hallie, who'd been looking at him with an odd expression as he'd been stroking the cat in her arms, snapped back to attention. "Oh, right. It means people to come in and help out around the shelter. Help with the animals." She bit her lip. "With no pay."

"Interesting," he said. Perhaps that would enable him to stay around the cat a bit longer. See if he could help him. Maybe that would fill something inside him.

The emptiness was killing him. Being able to heal again would soothe his soul.

That was if he could do it with his powers restrained.

He eyed Hallie. He needed to be careful with humans. He couldn't let himself get involved with them at all. If he started healing again, caring again, it would all go wrong. It was best if he went back to sleep before that could happen.

But maybe he could help the cat first. Maybe even the human a little, too.

"What's his name?" Luc asked.

"Bastien," she said, cocking her head.

"And if I volunteer here, I can see him?"

She nodded.

Her scent wafted toward him, violets and vanilla. Soothing and soft.

Would it really be so bad to get close to just one more human? Just for a little while?

"I'll take the job."

CHAPTER 2

Hallie blinked in shock. Men like this didn't come in here every day. In fact, the only one she'd seen this hot was Zach, the dark-haired guy who'd brought his friend in here.

But aside from their size and relative hottieness, the two were different as night and day.

This man's hair was a darker blond shot through with gold and little streaks of white, and his features were classically handsome, hard jaw, defined cheekbones, full lips, and thick, arched brows.

He kept distracting her with his eyes that were every color of sapphire, from the darkest midnight on the outer edge to a bright Caribbean-blue in the center, contrasting his pupils. And they were always changing, like dye in water.

But there was something in those eyes that struck her more than the colors. Loneliness. Maybe something even worse.

He was staring at her, making Bastien purr and relax when he'd never been at ease with anyone but her, and she realized this eccentric man just asked to volunteer.

"Wait," she said, even though the thought of working alongside a guy like this for even a few hours a week seemed like a dream come true. "I need to know your experience. I'll need a background check."

He frowned. "I can get them, but as you aren't paying me, is it really necessary?"

Zach appeared from behind him and walked forward with Hallie conspiratorially. "Do you think we could just not worry about it? He's kind of going through a rough time, just been through a big overseas move, and his stuff is everywhere."

"Do you have any experience with animals?" she asked.

He shrugged.

"You're going to have to be more helpful than that." She frowned.

"I... am a quick learner," he said quietly. "And I do like animals."

She swallowed. It was sort of against their rules, but strangely, she had a good feeling about this guy. And they needed the extra hands. Free help with those kinds of muscles wasn't exactly knocking on their door every day.

He'd be so useful for moving crates, heavy food, cages... and as eye candy.

She turned to put Bastien back in the cage, hiding her blush. She'd long ago stopped thinking about love, let alone with a guy that looked fit to grace a movie screen, not do manual labor around her shelter.

She could still feel the tingles in her body from when he'd been so close to her, touching Bastien and invading her space without realizing it. With the near constant pain she was in, it took a lot to distract her for even a moment.

But he had done just that. Was it only because he

was so hot her body went haywire? Or had there actually been some kind of soothing presence emanating from him?

She wasn't sure. She didn't have a lot of experience with hot guys. Her days were all work, and at night, she was exhausted and tired of dealing with people and just wanted to be home snuggling her cats.

But one thing she was sure of was there was something odd about this guy. Something that made her want to see more of him.

Literally, she thought, blushing again.

She looked up to see him watching her intently. He didn't look at her as any other guys did. Often, people made comments about her weight or sneered at her or dismissed her entirely. They had no idea what her life had been like. What she had fought or overcome.

All they saw was an overweight woman they could judge.

She liked her body. Was at home in it and grateful for it, and she wouldn't change herself for anything. All she would change was the critical look in people's eyes that said there was something wrong with her.

Except the handsome man in front of her didn't have that look in his eyes at all. In fact, if she hadn't been imagining it, she could swear she saw his eyes sweep over her, checking her out, and a slightly appreciative nod of his head.

But that was stupid. She was just daydreaming, because a man straight out of a superhero movie, with the most beautiful eyes she'd ever seen, happened to be staring at her.

She took a deep breath and made up her mind. She'd hire him, damn the consequences. She doubted Patty or Jenna would have a problem with their new volunteer once they laid eyes on him.

An unwelcome pang of possessiveness passed over her at that. A need to protect him from any gaze but hers.

Which was ridiculous. No man on earth had ever looked less like he needed protecting. Yet there was something vulnerable about him. Wounded almost.

She bit her lip. "When do you want to start?"

"And I can hang out with Bastien?" he asked.

"Sure," she said, still touched by how much he'd bonded with the little cat that no one else gave a second look.

"And if he were to get better, could I adopt him?" he asked, blue eyes hopeful.

A rock formed in her stomach. The last thing she wanted was for this man to grow attached when there was no hope. It wasn't a matter of "if" for Bastien, just a matter of "when."

"He's not going to get better," she said quietly. "But I'm sure he could use a friend."

The tall man cocked his head thoughtfully but didn't seem to really let it sink in.

"Injection site sarcoma is aggressive," she said. "I'm sorry. I want you to work here, but I don't want you to get your hopes up for nothing."

He sighed as he straightened and stretched. "I've had worse hopes before."

What did that mean?

Erin, Zach's kind, gentle wife, smiled at Hallie. "He's an odd one, but I think you can trust him."

Hallie laughed. "You think?"

Erin nodded. "I mean, no one's a sure bet."

Hallie turned to the giant man and tapped his arm. An electric shock zinged between them, and he raised an eyebrow, pursing his perfect lips at the contact.

She pulled back. "I don't even know your name," she said. "And we'll have to at least fill out an application. Well, you can take it home and bring it back with you."

"I'm Luc," he said flatly.

She led them back to the front office and grabbed a packet out of a drawer. When she went to hand it to him, she could swear his fingers lingered a little bit long on hers. Just a slight hesitation.

"You can start tomorrow," she said, struggling to speak when her throat had gone dry over how hot he was. Over the realization that he was actually coming there again.

"And you'll be here?" he asked, tucking the folded application in a pocket.

Her eyes widened. "Yes."

"Good," he said. And then he walked out with his

friends, pausing only to look over his shoulder and give a short wink. So quick she could have missed it.

Holy hell. Was this walking blond god actually into her?

* * *

Even though Luc told himself he was going back for the little hairless cat, Hallie's gray eyes were the foremost thing in his mind as he got ready for his first day at the shelter.

Zach and Erin had been surprised by his impetuous move to apply, but they were all too eager to get him out of the house.

He touched the collar around his neck, feeling the cold iron there.

Perhaps it was good his dragon was sealed. If it wasn't, he'd probably already be getting in trouble. Getting too involved. As it stood now, he could get to know humans and be out in the world without worrying about either side of his powers coming out.

On the one hand, he could be warm, caring, soothing. Able to heal and bring down rain. But the other side, the one that felt much closer to the surface since he'd awakened, was devastating, with icy blasts. Hard skin. Frozen projectiles. Blizzards.

Both should probably stay hidden for now. Maybe buried for the rest of time.

It was ironic that Zach was the one who'd managed to function in the human world and convince them to continue the experiment, waking up Luc.

Because Zac had never cared for humans in the time he'd been alive. Then again, he'd never killed them either.

And that was more than Luc could say.

Shame moved through him as he tied a tie over the dress shirt he'd found in Zach's closet. He wasn't sure of the dress code, but he wanted to look nice when seeing Hallie again, so he'd looked for the dressiest clothes.

"That's going to be overkill," Zach said, leaning against the door with a frown.

"I don't care," Luc said. "I'm going for the cat."

"Right, the cat," Zach said, raising an eyebrow with a cocky smile. "Sure." He straightened and walked to his dresser and pulled out a different set of clothes, still with tags on. "Here, try these. You'll fit in better."

Luc reluctantly changed into the light-blue sweater and dark jeans and sighed at how casual he appeared. He would never get used to modern clothing.

"Better?" he asked.

"Yup," Zach replied, coming into the room to look him over. "The 'cat' will be pleased. And anyone else you're aiming for…" He raised a questioning eyebrow.

"I don't know what you're talking about," Luc said sharply, messing with his hair, which wanted to stick in all directions.

"It looks fine," Zach said, shaking his head. "You're making it worse."

Luc stopped abruptly. "Are you here for a reason?"

"Just to make sure you don't look or act stupid out in the human world when I'm not there to supervise you."

"No one was around to supervise you," Luc said flatly.

"Erin sort of was." Zach grinned. "I got lucky

there."

"Yes, you did." Luc agreed. "But I'm fine on my own. I've been on my own a long time."

"Except you won't really be alone at all, will you?" Zach asked, a knowing gaze in his eyes.

Luc's stomach twisted slightly. "What are you talking about?"

"You know what I'm talking about. The little receptionist you were making eyes at."

"Making eyes?" he asked.

Zach sighed. "Ogling. Eye fucking."

"I beg your pardon," Luc said, disturbed.

"You found a human you like," Zach said, nudging him with a shoulder. "Good for you."

"It doesn't matter if I like her," Luc said. "Humans are not for mating."

Zach frowned. "What about me?"

Luc straightened his cuffs. "You seem to be making the impossible work. Which is the epitome of irony, considering the fact that you hated humans as a species not long ago."

"The world is different now," Zach said. "Give it

a chance."

Luc's eyes darted to the TV, which was covering another shooting. Always another shooting or fire or fight or war. "Doesn't seem so different to me."

"And you're different, too," Zach commented. "Maybe not in a good way, but you're definitely different."

He gave Luc a swat on the butt, and the tall man jumped back and glared at him. "What was that for?"

"To loosen you up," Zach said, striding out the door with his hands behind his head. "Now go get your mate."

Luc shook the thought from his head. He was going to stay uninvolved with humans. Sure, he could admire Hallie, enjoy her company, but that was it.

Anything further spelled disaster.

Still, a little uneasy part of him wondered, if she wasn't going to be his mate, why did he feel so obsessed with seeing her again?

He'd never felt that way about any creature. And looking at Zach, perhaps the expectation in this world was that dragons would take human mates.

Something that *never* would have been considered in his day.

He did know if he could pick one, someone like Hallie would be just his type. Hallie herself if possible.

But aside from her outward kindness, he'd seen no sign that she returned any of the attraction he felt. She'd only given him a smile and averted her eyes.

Too bad he wanted her to look right into him.

CHAPTER 3

Hallie glanced at the clock on the wall above her desk. It had little cat paws on it that moved with each tick of the second hand.

Two minutes to nine. Would he be late? Would he even show up? Would his good-looking friends convince him he really didn't need to volunteer at a shelter when he could walk into any agency and land a modeling contract?

She sighed and absentmindedly flipped her phone in her hand.

"When is the new volunteer coming again?" Patty asked hurriedly. "I still can't believe you hired him without asking any of us. We're all supposed to sign off." Patty was a pretty black woman with dark curls and eyes. She was heavier set, like Hallie, and had a sparkling personality when she wasn't stressed about work.

Which was most of the time.

Jenna, who'd been there the longest, was off today, which was probably fine. She didn't really like guys much—though Hallie wasn't sure if she liked girls either—and she would only make Lucien's day more awkward.

Which it already would be. He had this ethereal look to him, almost like he wasn't from this world and needed to be protected, despite his height and the sense of power radiating off of him.

Still, Hallie knew better than most that there were more strengths than just the physical.

The door to the shelter dinged as a man's tall shadow blocked the bright morning light streaming through the doorway.

"That must be him," Patty said.

Hallie put up a hand. The three seconds it took Luc to walk through the second set of doors and into the florescent light where she could see him were the longest of her life.

"Holy Moses," Patty breathed out, putting a hand through her hair and leaning back in her chair, making it creak. "What the heck is *he* doing here?"

Hallie bit her lip, fighting her own reaction as a wave of attraction rippled through her. "He really likes one of the cats."

"Smoking hot and loves animals? My-*lanta*." Patty fanned herself, and Hallie stood to walk around the counter to greet him.

Once again, she was impressed by how impossibly tall he was. Intimidating, though the expression on his stunningly handsome face was mostly neutral. The angles of his cheekbones and jaw and nose appeared plotted by someone who was trying to draw the most beautiful male visage possible.

His eyes looked astounding with the blue sweater he wore. A sweater that skimmed the bulging muscles of his tall body, making her mouth water.

She liked a hot guy as much as the next one, but she'd never had a reaction like this.

She wiped her sweaty palms on her skirt before holding out a hand for him to shake. When he took her hand, he simply held it for a moment, gazing down at her with an unreadable expression as he looked her over.

And then that expression was readable, the blue eyes mercurial. Heat. Want.

Was that even possible?

She pulled back, and he let her go, cocking his head as if he weren't sure what he'd done wrong.

"You pulled back," he said. "Was I hurting you?"

"No," she said. In fact, it had felt good touching him, like something warm and soothing was flowing through her. But it had been too intense, and she'd felt as if her legs were going to melt right out from underneath her if he stared at her with those blue flame eyes any longer.

She stepped back, adjusting her clothes. As her eyes skimmed up him, she couldn't believe how long his legs were and how the wide, strong muscles there filled in his jeans.

She looked up and saw a slight smile quirking the

side of his full lips, and she caught her breath. It was like seeing just the slightest hint of sunlight peeking out from behind a cloud, and she could just imagine how beautiful all the rays would be if it could just come out farther.

But as quickly as he'd smiled, it was gone, hidden behind a handsome mask of indifference once again.

"So what should I start with?" he asked.

She bit her lip and folded her arms. Normally, they'd ask the new volunteers to clean cages to get used to the place, but if she asked that of this clean-looking, gorgeous male who looked like he'd never gotten his hands dirty in his life, would he run?

Then she wouldn't be able to see him again, and she'd never been so intrigued by a human being in her life.

Still, she should treat him like anyone else. Maybe she could help him with the cages and that would make it better.

Or are you just trying to spend more time with him because he smells so damn good?

"First, we clean cages."

"Girl, that man doesn't need to clean no cages!" Patty shouted, and Hallie just grinned as she led Luc to the back.

"Ignore her," she said as Luc glanced curiously over his shoulder.

"I'm Patty," she called out. "And you're heaven to look at!"

"Heaven?"

"You don't know what heaven is?" Hallie asked as she opened the door to the back.

Luc held the door for her, giving her a hint of his spicy scent as she walked through, brushing by his body and suppressing a shiver.

"No, I know what heaven is. I don't know why she says I'm heaven to look at."

"She just means you're pretty is all."

He sat on a bench while she pulled cleaning supplies out of a cupboard. "I thought women were pretty."

"Some men are, too," she said, averting her eyes as she gestured for him to follow her to the first set of cages. She gently began lifting animals out, putting them in a temporary holding area where they could play while she cleaned.

He crouched beside them, watching them play. "I don't think there is anything particularly feminine about me."

She gave him a placating smile. "I don't either." She sprayed down the inside of the cage and began to wipe it clean. "I think some women just use it to mean really good-looking. Very attractive. Sexy."

She was spraying again when she felt the bottle lifted out of her hands. She looked up as he opened a cage next to her and began working with it, taking his own rag to it.

Then he looked over at her, blue eyes inquisitive. "Do you think I'm really good-looking? Very attractive? Sexy?" He grinned as he repeated her words, and she felt butterflies flutter to life in her stomach.

She laughed nervously. "What do you think?"

He cocked his head. "I don't know. That's why I'm asking you."

"Of course I think you're attractive," she said, because she saw no point in lying. It would be like telling the sun it wasn't shiny.

"Interesting," he said. "I had no idea."

"You didn't?" she asked.

"Of course not. I didn't read your mind." He went back to scrubbing.

But it bothered her, the way he'd said that. Almost as if he were saying he *could* have read her mind but chose *not* to.

A little chill rippled up her arms as she began work on another cage, removing the little bowls and bedding so she could put them back after. "So, um…" She trailed off. How did one even ask a handsome man about whether he could read minds? She decided she was just reading too far into it and decided to drop the subject.

"So, um, where are you from, then?"

He looked over at her, his blue eyes so bright near the center and so dark on the outside that they stood out incredibly from his face. "Somewhere else."

"Oh," she said as he stood up and walked over to Bastien's cage, running his finger over the lock.

"Do you mind if I get him out?" he asked.

"Sure." Normally it wouldn't be time for a break, but he was a volunteer, and besides, it was interesting to watch this mysterious man interact with animals.

She sat on a bench, dropping her rag back in a bucket and letting herself rest for a moment as she watched Luc.

He opened the cage carefully, and once again, Bastien lit up like he never did for anyone other than Hallie. The graceful, exotic-looking cat slinked into Luc's arms and immediately purred, turning onto his back and rubbing his cheek against Luc's arm.

She could swear she saw a slight smile on Luc's face as he watched the little cat make himself comfortable. Luc raised a hand and stroked over the cat's cheeks, and Bastien's eyes closed in relief. Soon, the purring stopped; Bastien was asleep.

Hallie couldn't believe what she was seeing. One of the grumpier, most nervous cats in the shelter was behaving like a perfect lap cat. Not to mention acting as if not in any pain at all. They tried to keep Bastien medicated, but it had never given him relief or relaxation like this.

"There, there," Luc muttered in a low voice. "Does that feel better?" He stroked over the cat's head. "I guess I haven't lost my touch."

She walked up behind him quietly, looking over at Bastien. "You're magical," she said. "I've never seen anything like this with him."

Luc just shrugged, his attention still on the cat as he gave him soothing strokes over his head and face, just where most cats liked to be touched.

"So what other magical powers do you have?" she asked, watching him in amusement.

"Magical powers?" he asked, his hand freezing on the cat as he stared at her in confusion.

"It was a joke." She walked over to nudge him in the side. "Geez, you need to lighten up."

"Lighten up," he said skeptically. "I keep hearing that. Not sure what there is to lighten up about with the world going to hell."

She looked up at him in surprise. What a gloomy thing to hear from someone who seemed like he had it all together. Money, looks, privilege. What did he have to complain about?

Still, she knew from personal experience that you could have wounds no one saw.

"So many things to lighten up about," she said. "Sunny days like today. Cute animals getting adopted." She reached out to stroke a cat. "Nice people coming in to volunteer." She peeked at the clock. "Yummy lunch in just a few hours."

"It doesn't take much to please you, does it?" he asked, amused.

She shook her head. "Nope. I'm a pretty happy person." Just as she said it, a tiny spark of pain shot through her, reverberating down her spine. She fought back a wince. The aching had been better for some reason last night and this morning, so she'd skipped a bout of meds.

Now she needed to go get them.

"I'll be right back," she said, rising carefully, hiding her limp.

"Are you feeling okay?" he asked, concerned.

She glared at him. It was odd that he asked that now, almost as if he'd sensed it. She was good at hiding her pain. No one ever asked her about it. But somehow this man saw through her mask. She narrowed her eyes. Maybe he really could read minds?

"I'm fine," she said, waving a hand. "You just keep working."

She didn't mean to sound curt, but she wasn't used to having people pick up on her discomfort. Oftentimes, it was just at the back of her mind.

But he was the last person she wanted looking at her with pity. She'd go take her meds, do some quick meditation to relax and lessen the muscle spasms, and then she'd get back to work.

She'd meant what she'd said. There were too many good things in life to focus on the negative.

She just hoped she could show him the same.

CHAPTER 4

Luc was getting more and more confused about this Hallie person. As they ate lunch across from each other at the table, once again he got the feeling that she hadn't a care in the world.

But the occasional waves of pain from her meant that wasn't true.

It had to be impressive pain to come over the high barriers he'd erected against feeling any empathy for anyone. Or maybe he was sensing it more because he was starting to become more connected to her.

Not to mention attracted to her.

Today, her dark hair was swept into a tidy ponytail, bringing more emphasis to her pretty, heart-shaped face and big, expressive eyes.

She was wearing a light-purple sweater that made her gray eyes reflect lilac and soft-looking jeans that hugged her generous curves.

As she ate her sandwich and babbled about things to do with the shelter, events coming up, stuff like that, he longed to be able to ask her more personal things. Like what had happened to her and why she wasn't angry about it.

But perhaps it wasn't the right time.

She set down her sandwich when she noticed he wasn't eating his. She nudged it toward him, still wrapped in its paper. "Hey, something wrong? You aren't eating."

No, but he was feasting. Feasting on how beautiful she was and how much light and hope she radiated.

It was slowly affecting the gloom inside him, making the ice seem that much less impenetrable.

"You don't talk much, do you?" she asked.

He shook his head and began to unwrap the sandwich. "I don't have much to say."

She tilted her head, making her soft, brown hair spill over one shoulder. She probably had no idea how sexy that was. "I'm sure you do, although I'm not sure I'd want to hear it. What were you saying about the world going to hell?"

He leaned back in his chair, taking a bite of the sandwich to give him time to think. The sandwich was fine, though food didn't taste good anymore. Erin had said that was a sign of depression, but he wasn't depressed, right?

Just tired of the world.

"You think it isn't?" he asked, truly curious.

She rested her cheek on her hand. "I think there are lots of good things in it. Lots of good people. I like most people I meet. Like you."

He nodded. "But what about the TV? Everything on the news?"

"They like to focus on the bad," she said.

"Still, it seems like there is a lot of bad to focus on," he said.

"Maybe." She sighed. "But the worse it gets, the more important it is for good people to step up and fight for what's right. Bad things happening is a reason for good people to become active, not disgusted."

Active. Like he and the other dragons had been. But still, she was a human. Of course she would feel that way about her race. Of course she would see things with rose-colored glasses.

She hadn't seen what humans could do to other humans.

"Anyway, if you're so hopeless about life, what are you doing here?" she asked. "This kind of place is so depressing most people can't stand it."

He looked in the direction of the back room full of cages. "I want to help Bastien."

"See?" she said, putting her hands up. "That's what I mean. Other people stay engaged with the world for the same reason you stay engaged with the shelter. Because there are people we love there."

Love. There was a word. If he stayed around long enough, would she come to love *him*?

Maybe not if she ever found out what he was. What he *did*.

"You're staring again," she said, her pale cheeks

flushing prettily. "You keep doing that, and I don't get what you mean by it. Are you trying to make me feel awkward? You know, girls like me aren't used to being stared at by—"

He cut her off with a kiss, leaning across the table. He didn't know exactly what provoked it. Maybe he just wanted to stop the hurt, hesitant words spilling from her lips. Maybe he wanted to end that wary look in her eyes.

Or maybe he just sensed somehow that she wanted him as much as he wanted her.

The way she melted into the kiss and wrapped her arms around him certainly seemed to say as much.

He reached up to touch her hair, pulling a few strands free from the ponytail, the softest thing he'd ever felt. Would her skin be even softer?

She sighed as he trailed his hand down to cup her neck, rubbing his thumb lightly over her pulse.

She was special. He could feel it even more as he kissed her, touched her. He needed more of her. More and more. He couldn't stop looking at her. Couldn't stop touching her. Felt caught up in something that was above him, for the first time in his life.

He deepened the kiss, parting her lips and diving inside to taste her, sealing their mouths together in a hot embrace, as his other hand came up to cup her face.

The shelter disappeared; the modern world disappeared. There was only him and the most beautiful woman in the world and feelings between them that didn't make any sense.

When he pulled back, gazing into her dazed gray eyes, he felt as if he were floating slowly back to ground after soaring somewhere high.

He looked down at her lips, slightly swollen. She sat back in her chair, putting a hand over her heart.

He knew it was racing. He'd felt it.

Despite all his promises not to engage with another human, he was connecting with one more deeply than ever before. Even worse, it was effortless. Worst of all? He wanted more of it.

It was stupid, but maybe it really was a new world. Maybe things were possible that hadn't been before.

He felt something small and flickering awakening

inside him. Something he hadn't felt in a long time.

Hope.

"That was…" She trailed off, touching her lips. "What *was* that?"

He leaned back, making his chair creak. "I don't know." But he did. It was claiming. It was soothing. It was to tell her there was nothing in his stare but admiration and an instant kind of caring that made no sense to him.

As if he could see her soul and it bonded him to her.

He stood. He needed to go talk to Zach about this. Was this how he'd felt when he met Erin?

"I… don't know what to say," she said.

He just watched her, waiting for any reaction. He'd made a bold move, and he wasn't sure how she'd take it now that the heat of the moment was gone. Or was it? His body was still stirring in anticipation of more.

So odd to feel that for a human.

"I… um… So what now?" she asked. "I mean, I had no idea you… Why did you kiss me again?"

"Because I wanted to," he said. "I've been wanting to since I met you. Truthfully, I took this job in part because I wanted to see you."

She swallowed and then smiled. "To see me?"

He nodded.

She sighed and slumped back in her chair. "You didn't have to volunteer just to see me."

"I wanted to see Bastien, too. But I'd be lying if I said you didn't play a role in my decision. You affect me in a way no one ever has."

"I don't even know you," she said, touching a hand to her lips.

"You could, though, if you wanted to," he said.

"How?" she asked.

"Do you ever spend time with people outside of work?"

"Like a date?" she asked.

He cocked his head, unsure what that was exactly. "A date?"

"Yeah, you know, a guy and a girl going out romantically."

Hmm. He wasn't sure if that was exactly what he

wanted. He just wanted to get to know her. Find out why she had this zest for life and if she could bring him out of the frozen wasteland he'd been inhabiting for so long.

But he guessed, based on the kiss, that he also felt romantic enough for a date.

"Yes, a date," he said. "That works."

She rolled her eyes, but a smile quirked her lips. "I guess you're really excited."

"I don't know what you mean."

"You know, the hesitation," she said.

"I'm not from around here," he explained. "Sometimes I'm going to be awkward."

"Where are you from, then?" she asked, but he ignored the question.

"How do we arrange this date?" he said, standing and stretching.

"You should probably take my number," she suggested, holding out her phone.

Right. Phones. The things humans used for everything. He pulled his out of his pocket and tried to remember the lock code. He tried a few and then finally succeeded. Then he handed it to her. "Can you put it in?"

She did. "Can I put yours in mine?"

"Of course," he said. "But I never use it."

She smiled. "That'll change as you get used to it."

He sort of doubted it. He could think of a million better things to do than stare at a phone.

Unless she was calling. Then he'd stay glued to it.

Oh hell, what was happening to him? Was it possible she was melting the ice dragon inside him?

"There," she said, handing back his cell. "Now you can call me. And take me out tonight, if you want to."

Of course he wanted to. He wanted to be with her, take her out, talk to her until he understood everything about her, stay with her until he was inside her soul.

"I want to," he answered resolutely.

She stood and gave him a hug, wrapping her arms around him. "Well, whatever happens, I'm really glad you came in." She checked the clock. "You're off for now. You only had a half shift today. So just text me when you decide what you want to do."

"Okay," he said. "Will do."

He turned to go, but his body was reluctant to leave her. He felt frozen in place, wanting to stay as close as possible. To protect her.

But he needed to go home, needed to rest and get some advice for tonight.

It was crucial he spend more time with her. He needed to find out if she was really the key to everything changing inside him or just a distraction that would turn end up in heartbreak again.

Like the last time he cared for humans.

"See you," she said, snapping him out of his fog.

"See you." He walked backward toward the door, wanting to keep his eye on her as long as possible.

Then he turned and let himself out into the afternoon sunshine, bringing a hand up to protect his eyes.

After just one day with her, the world already felt different. Gentle or not, this was one powerful human.

CHAPTER 5

Zach and Erin were making lunch in the kitchen when Luc walked in, hands in pockets, deep in thought about seeing Hallie again that night.

"You're home early," Zach said, taking off oven mitts to walk over to him and give him a half hug.

Luc winced. Zach was already picking up so many human habits. Like being friendly. "I worked a half shift."

"Thought you would want to work all day, considering the cute little lady next to you," Erin teased from her spot at the counter, stirring something in a large bowl. "Have you eaten?"

He nodded. He'd finished the sandwich on the

way home. "Are you about to eat? I need advice from Zach."

"Hey," Erin said. "I'm the emotionally intelligent one. I should be the one giving advice."

She had a point. She was also a human woman. He would get both of their advice, then.

"Okay," he said, sitting down at a chair and stretching. The chairs here were bigger than at the shelter. Much more dragon sized. "I need to know about taking a human on a date."

Zach let out a bark of a laugh. "Yeah," he said. "I'm glad you're asking Erin on this one, because I thought the way to ask a woman out was to tell her I was a dragon and she was fortunate to be chosen by me."

She snorted. "It was sort of charming, in a completely *wrong* kind of way." She lifted her shoulders. "Then again, now that I know you weren't crazy, I guess it's kind of romantic how quickly you knew."

He swung an arm around her waist and pulled her in for a quick kiss. "Instantly, baby."

"Ugh," Luc said. "So human."

They both laughed at that and went on kissing, ignoring him. He averted his eyes, waiting for them to be done so someone could answer his question.

Then again, he thought, peeking back at them. If he went out with Hallie, would he end up with something like they had? Not what he'd ever pictured wanting as a dragon, but it didn't seem too bad now.

Kissing Hallie had definitely been something.

Zach pulled back abruptly and stared at his friend. "Ew. Stop thinking about kissing while I'm trying to make out with my wife."

"Stop making out with your wife while I'm sitting at your kitchen table," Luc retorted. "And get out of my mind."

Zach snorted. "Dragon thoughts. Hard to ignore."

Erin, however, pushed forward and sat across from Luc. "Oh my gosh, you kissed her already?"

"I did," he said. "It was nice."

"Whoa," Zach said, sitting down by his mate. "Start at the beginning."

So Luc did, telling them all about holding Bastien

and the shelter and the other worker and their conversation and lunch...

"Get to the kiss," Zach snapped.

So Luc did, telling them about the way she'd misunderstood his staring and how he'd surprised himself by going for it. And how they'd exchanged numbers.

"So you haven't set a time or anything?" Erin said.

"I needed help knowing more about dates first," Luc said.

"You came to the right place," Zach said, putting his hands behind his head.

Erin smirked. "Says the guy who used 'I'm an immortal dragon' as a pickup line."

"Yeah." Zach looked thoughtful. "Did you try that?"

Luc stifled a smile. "No."

"Thank heavens for that." Erin chuckled.

"Hey, it worked for you," Zach said.

"No," Erin said. "Getting to know you worked for me. I had to try to just not think about all the crazy dragon stuff."

Zach pouted. "Crazy dragon stuff? How about *awesome* dragon stuff?"

"Back to me," Luc said. "Help."

Erin grinned. "Right. What do you want to do together?"

"Do?" he asked. "I thought we were just being together."

"It's a date. You have to do something. Spend some money."

"I don't have access to my treasure," he said flatly.

"You can have some of Zach's," Erin said, noting Zach's scowl. "I'm kidding. Look, you can borrow anything you need from us. Money. A car. Can you drive?"

"I took a course at the oracle's place," he said. "I believe I'm sufficient."

Zach and Erin looked at each other. "Well," Zach said. "I guess it's a good thing we have a Volvo." They both laughed.

"What?" Luc asked.

"Nothing," Erin said. "So does she want you to pick her up at work or wait until she gets home and has time to get ready?"

Luc blanched. "I don't know. Do I need to call her and ask her all of this?" This was getting more complicated than he imagined.

"You could text," Erin said.

"Text?" Luc asked.

"You know, write something and send it, and then she sends something back."

"Like letters?" he asked. "Why would you do that when you have telephones and can hear each other's voice?"

"Because it's easier. Unlock your phone and I'll show you."

Luc sighed but pushed the phone over. Erin had been nothing but a good person to him. Despite her being human, he could trust her.

She took his phone and hit the keys rapidly and then handed it back to him. "Easy. See?"

He looked down at the screen. Next to his avatar, which the oracle had jokingly set as a fat little blue cartoon dragon, was a bubble with words inside.

Do you want me to pick you up from work or at your place? And what time is good?

He looked at Erin. "Now what?"

"Now we wait," she said.

"See?" he said in frustration. "I told you we should have called. It would be instant—" He was cut off by a beep from his phone and a little bubble appearing beside a photo of a cat.

How about seven at my place? Then she had listed an address.

His heart thumped. That was fast. Maybe this texting thing wasn't so bad.

"So I can send her anything this way?" he asked.

"Just don't send anything you care about someone else seeing," Erin said. "That is going over the internet."

"Right, keep secrets off of it, then," he said.

"Yeah, I wouldn't go announcing you're a dragon," she said. "Unless you're Zach."

Luc snorted. "Thank you for being patient with me. It's more than I deserve."

"Hey," Luc said. "We're friends. And besides, you can help save the world. We're going to need you with Emerald out there, plotting with whoever helped him escape."

"It's disappointing," Luc said. "I know he was always jealous of you and that his powers kind of leaned to the darker side of things, but I didn't expect him to completely turn like this."

"Yeah," Zach said.

"It hasn't been the same since Opal," Luc said.

"Yeah," Zach repeated, and a somber mood fell over the room.

"What is Opal?" Erin asked, glancing between them.

Neither spoke, and Luc looked down at the phone screen. He tapped on the text part and began to type.

Seven is good. I will pick you up. In a car.

He ignored Zach and Erin, who were having an awkward moment, and waited for her response. Since he hadn't sent a question, would she still say something?

Great. Cars are much preferable to spaceships.

Or tricycles. ;)

He handed the phone to Erin. "What on earth is she talking about?"

Erin laughed. "She's just teasing you. You didn't need to specify you were picking her up in a car. There isn't really any other way."

"If I were in dragon form, I could pick her up with dragon wings."

Erin laughed. "Okay. But you aren't in dragon form. So just know most humans assume car."

"Fine," he said, suddenly thinking about how fun it would be to be partially shifted, flying with Hallie in his arms. Kissing the sky, clouds swirling around him, sheltering her in his wings so they could be truly alone up there…

"Dude," Zach said. "With thoughts like that, she really might be your mate."

Luc blinked. Perhaps Zach had a point. Despite him never thinking of a mate as a possibility, he had to admit that if he had ever guessed what it would feel like to have one, it would probably be something like this obsession with Hallie.

"What should I send back?" he asked, emboldened and wanting to flirt.

"Tell her you'll leave your spaceship at home," Erin joked.

"Tell her you can still bring the tricycle," Zach said.

But Luc paused, wanting to come up with his own statement. "Got it," he said, typing on his phone. He hit send and then handed it to Erin and Zach to read.

Doesn't matter what we go in as long as I go with you.

Zach snorted. "That's um… not really teasing. That's more…"

"Sincere," Erin said. "I guess now we wait and see if it works."

Luc guessed he didn't understand teasing, but it didn't matter. He didn't have time for silly games. He just needed to get closer to this intriguing human.

The phone beeped.

"I have to know what she said to that," Zach said.

Luc looked down at the phone.

You are so sweet. I'll see you in a few hours. PS:

I like your dragon avatar. Dragons are the best, aren't they?

He smiled, a full, genuine smile that he felt warming him from his toes to the top of his head.

What had he done to deserve meeting this human? Or more accurately, what had he been forgiven for?

He closed out the bad memories and focused on the phone.

He was here. This was a new world, a new him. A new life.

One more chance to make things right.

See you tonight.

* * *

While waiting on Hallie's doorstep, Luc was so nervous that his palms were starting to get sweaty.

And the idea of a sweaty dragon was extremely unseemly, so he hoped she opened the door soon.

When she did, his jaw dropped. He'd never seen her wear anything like this before. It was a formfitting dress in a soft, casual material that ended just below her dimpled knees, with sleeves to her elbows. But in the front, it dipped, showing a fair amount of soft, plump cleavage, pressed together deliciously.

Good heavens, with the skin showing, soft arms, curvy legs, and that gorgeous face, he was going to have his hands full trying not to kill men who looked at her.

And then her hair. She'd taken it down and curled it in soft waves around her face, and she was wearing something on her face to enhance her eyelashes, making them darker and sultrier. She was wearing flat shoes in a shiny leather, and he was relieved to see it was easy for her to walk.

"You look amazing," he said, putting out an arm for her as he'd seen chivalrous humans do back in his time.

She smiled, so bright it almost blinded him, and put her arm around his. Soft and warm. He nearly melted at her touch, but he led her down to the black car he'd been lent for the drive over. He opened her door as Erin had shown him and waited until she was in to go around to his side.

When he was in and the door was closed, he sat

there for a second just staring at her, wondering how he was supposed to focus on anything but this gorgeous woman beside him.

"You okay?" she asked. "We don't have to do this if you're uncomfortable."

He raised an eyebrow. "Uncomfortable?" His eyes roamed over her. "That's not what I'm feeling."

She squirmed, and he found himself mesmerized by the movement of her body.

Snap out of it, Luc. You have things to do.

"So, um, we're going for ice cream," he said. It had seemed the safest of the options Zach and Erin had suggested. Mud wrestling had been on this list.

"Oh," she said, looking down at her outfit. "Am I overdressed?"

"If anything, I'd say underdressed," he said bluntly.

Her face fell. "You don't like it?"

He bit the inside of his cheek. "I love it." The last thing he wanted was to hurt her. Sure, he'd have to try to keep himself from punching every man who looked at her all night, but it was worth it for her to wear whatever she wanted to. "I just know you're going to get a lot of attention, and I want you all to myself."

Her eyes were wide with surprise as she looked over at him. "What planet are you from?"

"This one. Why?" he said flatly.

She folded her arms over herself cautiously. "I just don't get that kind of attention."

"Maybe you do and you just don't notice it," he said.

"Maybe you are biased," she retorted. "Maybe you're the only one looking."

"That would suit me just fine," he said, glancing over to see she was blushing.

She sighed. "This is what makes me think you're from another world sometimes. Look, guys who look like you don't say things like that to girls like me."

"I think you're the one who's coming down to my level," he said, reaching out to tilt her chin to make her look at him. "You're a good person. An amazing person. And you're beautiful, too." He let her see the heat in his gaze. "And if others don't look at you, they are fools. And if they do look at you, I'll try not to kill them."

She let out a shaky breath, fanning her face as she sat back. "Whew. You're seriously something."

"I think you are something," he said. "And I think you don't give yourself enough credit."

"I like myself," she said. "But sometimes people just don't understand. And they bully. And that stuff sticks with you." She gave him a rueful smile. "But I'll try not to think about that and just enjoy a date with the hottest guy in the world."

He was busy thinking of all the ways to kill her bullies when he realized she had called him hot, and a huge grin spread over his face. "Hottest?"

She shifted away with a giggle. "Stop fishing for compliments."

He did, focusing on the road as he drove to the small ice cream shop Zach and Erin had recommended.

When they arrived, he made sure to go around to her side and open the door, helping her out.

As they walked across the parking lot, he held her hand, enjoying the contrast of her closeness with the cool air of the night.

It was empty out here, save for a few cars, and he realized he could have parked closer, but he was glad since it gave him the opportunity to hold her hand a while longer.

When they came to the counter, she was swinging her hand in his while ordering, and then he felt a small wave of pain.

She stepped back slightly, and he looked over in concern. "Sorry," she said. "I think I need to go sit down. I'll go save a booth for us." She took a cup from the cashier, gave him an apologetic glance, and went to sit down.

He finished their order and waited by the counter, keeping an eye on her while not openly staring. He knew her pain was a point of pride for her, something she didn't want people poking their noses into, but he was getting to the point where he felt he needed to know more.

So he could help her in whatever way he could.

He flexed his hands, wishing he had his dragon power flowing through him.

Out of the corner of his eye, he saw Hallie take

out a small container and pop something in her mouth, which she then washed down with a gulp of water.

Medicine most likely.

Cold moved through him. Whatever was wrong with her, was it serious? Was it just an old injury, or was it something like Bastien?

He shook the thoughts from his mind. They brought back old fears, and he didn't want that.

When their ice creams were ready, he brought them over to Hallie and set them on the table. She gave him a big smile, seeming as if she were doing better.

But Luc wondered how much pain he'd be feeling from her if he had access to his full empathy rather than icy walls around his heart with only tiny cracks in them.

She took her ice cream from him, giving him a big smile as she dug into it. "Ah," she said, sighing. "It's the little things in life."

He wanted to ask her how the little things could matter so much when something else really sucked. But he was too busy being enchanted by how happy she looked when she ate.

He wished he could learn to just live in the moment like that. Instead, the past and the future hung over his head constantly, waiting to drop like heavy, punishing weights.

She licked a drop of her ice cream slowly off her full lower lip, and he felt his heart pick up a beat.

She was so beautiful. Watching her happy, watching her enjoy anything was bliss.

"You're staring at me again," she said. "I told you it makes me feel awkward when you—"

He slid into the booth next to her, surprising her, and caught her lips with his own. She calmed, sinking into the kiss, and put a hand up to touch his hair.

Amazing.

When he pulled back, she was quiet and ready to listen. He brushed a loose wave of hair back from her face. "Of course I'm staring at you. I *like* you. I have from the moment I saw you. You intrigue me unlike anyone else ever has."

"Why?" she asked.

There were so many reasons. He could tell her it was because she was beautiful and kind, but it was more than that. It felt... fated. Like she'd been destined to help his dragon come back to life.

But he couldn't tell her that. "I'm still figuring that out."

"I guess you're honest at least," she said, smiling as she turned her attention back to her ice cream.

Honest. The word burned at him as he pulled his ice cream over to him and swirled his spoon it in, stirring it up. He couldn't even begin to be honest with her yet, and it was starting to bug him.

He was starting to wonder if Zach had the right idea all along in just blurting everything out, when he saw a group of men come in the door and turned his attention toward them.

He didn't like the way one of them was looking at his date.

CHAPTER 6

"Luc? Luc?" she asked for the third time as she tried to pull her handsome date's focus back to her.

She still couldn't believe she was here with him, his attention all on her in a way that was so foreign and pleasant she was afraid to even hope it was real.

Would she wake up tomorrow and find out it was all just a dream?

His body looked amazing in a slim tee shirt that fit his biceps perfectly and showed off large, square pecs and rippling abs. It was light blue, enhancing his eyes, not that they needed any enhancement.

And then there was how amazing his ass looked in his jeans. She resisted the urge to fan her face as she remembered watching him at the counter. She'd been so excited for her date that she'd forgotten to take meds again, so she'd had to take them here. Oddly, forgetting her meds seemed to be happening more and more lately.

She wasn't sure why. Maybe hot dudes were a natural form of painkiller.

She giggled at the thought and looked over to see Luc still glaring at the group in the corner, so she sighed and nudged his arm again. "Luc?"

"What?" he asked, not looking at her.

"Are you okay?"

His entire demeanor had changed when he'd seen the group of guys enter the parlor. They looked a little rough, but this place wasn't in the nicest part of town. It was set up like a fifties diner and served things other than ice cream, so it wasn't that unusual for a group of guys to be grabbing food.

But Luc didn't seem to get that. If he'd been a cat, he'd have had his hackles up. He looked even bigger than usual as he stared over at the group in the corner.

"Hey," she said, placing a hand on his arm. "What on earth is bothering you?"

He pulled his eyes away from the group and glared at the table. "Disgusting men." He shook his head. "Humans are disgusting."

"What do you mean?" she asked.

"Their thoughts," he said.

There he went again, implying he could read minds or something. "How would you know what they're thinking?"

For a moment, he looked confused. Then he shook his head. "I'm a man, aren't I? I know what men are thinking." He rolled his full lips together, then took a deep breath and relaxed a little. "But I'm being rude. I'm sorry."

"Come on," she said, taking his hand between hers and warming it. It felt so cold. "Don't worry about them. Tell me more about you."

"Okay," he said hesitantly, clearly trying to resist looking back at the group.

"Why do you have a dragon as your avatar on your phone?"

"A friend put that in for me," he said. "I didn't pick it."

"Aw," she said. "I love dragons."

"Yeah, you said that. Why?"

"I play games online sometimes. And read fantasy books. Dragons are always the best characters."

He laughed. "Are they? How so?"

"Super strong," she said. "Usually badass and cool with great powers."

"Hm," he said. "Are they?"

"Yeah," she said. "Do you play any games? Wait, no, I forgot. You don't even use your phone. Stupid question. So what do you do in your free time?"

He bit his lip. It was full and slightly pink, and she wanted to be the one biting him. "I don't do really anything right now."

"That's a shame," she said. "So many fun things to do. So before you moved, what did you do for a living?"

He thought about it. "Security, I guess."

"How so?"

"I was a bodyguard, maybe?"

That made sense with his tall build. "Why did you stop?"

"I was fired."

"Why?" she asked.

He leaned closer to her in the booth and pulled her against him. "Don't worry about it."

She pushed away. "No, I will worry about it. You're so vague about everything you tell me. What about your family?"

"Dead," he said.

"Right," she said. "Of course. So you can't tell me where you lived before or what you specifically did or anything about your family, other than they're dead."

He ran a hand through his sun-streaked, dark-blond hair. "I can tell you anything else, though."

"Why did your friend put a dragon as an avatar?" she asked. "I assumed you were a gamer or something."

He shrugged his massive shoulders. "I don't know. You'd have to ask her."

She sighed, leaning over her ice cream bowl. "Sometimes I feel like you're so distant. And then you kiss me, and I feel so close. Like I know you. None of this makes any sense."

"You're telling me," he said.

"Why?" she asked. "I'm an open book to you. Everything should make sense to you. You're the one in control."

"What is your family like?" he asked.

"Splintered," she said. "My dad divorced my mom when I was young. He made a new family with another wife. My mom and I aren't that close. She had to work a lot while I was growing up. I'm closer to my sister, but she lives overseas with her army husband. So I guess I'm pretty much alone." She smiled sadly. "See? I'm an open book."

"Then why do you hide your pain?" he asked as blatant as the nose on her face.

Her jaw dropped slightly in shock. Had she been that obvious? No one ever really noticed. "I… I guess I'm just used to it."

He folded his arms. "What happened?"

"I'm not sure it's any of your business," she said. "But I was in an accident."

"A car accident?" he asked.

She nodded.

"So nothing like Bastien?"

"No." She confirmed. "I'm not dying, if that's what you're worrying about."

He frowned. "I just... can sense your pain. Usually people don't hide it."

She raised an eyebrow. "How would you know if they were?"

He shrugged, looking over at the group for a moment before turning back to her. "I just can sometimes."

"Sometimes, but not all the time," she said.

"I think that's one of the things that draws me to you," he said. "Your constant positivity. It's such a mystery to someone like me, who can't seem to let go of anything bad that happens."

"I guess I just choose to be happy. To see the good things in life," she said.

"How did it happen?" he asked.

"I was hit by a drunk driver," she said. "Ten years ago. It kind of... ended everything back then. But I found a new life. It wasn't all bad."

His expression went dark. "So someone hurt you, probably nearly killed you, because they were stupid."

Was it her imagination or had the air gone colder by a few degrees? Possibly just the ice cream inside her, she guessed. "Luc, it was a long time ago."

"How do you just forget it?"

"I don't forget," she said. "I just don't let it ruin me." She sighed.

"I knew when it happened, I had two choices. To be incredibly unhappy and angry at the unfairness of it, or to be happy I still had my life."

"But it shouldn't have happened," he said.

"You can say that about a lot of things in life," she said. "Like Bastien's cancer or my parent's divorce or the shootings on the news. But in the end, there are so many good things in life that make it worthwhile."

"Like what?" he asked, folding his arms and leaning on the table. His eyes were starting to wander back to the other table again, so she had to distract him.

"Sunny days. Cute animals. Knowing you're making a difference in the world." She took a bite. "Delicious ice cream. Good company." She looked into his eyes. "Sexy guys."

That got a smile out of him. "Think I'm sexy, huh?"

"Yeah," she said. "And a good date."

He grinned, but his eyes wandered to the corner again.

"Maybe we should go," she said. "It seems like you're getting antsy."

"I just don't have a high opinion of people. I don't trust them around things that are precious to me."

Her heart fluttered like paper in the wind. She was precious to him? She tried to remember what they were talking about. Oh, right. Assuming the worst. "If other humans are worrying you, then let's just get away from them."

"Yeah," he said. "I was just hoping they would leave first. I don't like how they are thinking—I mean, *looking* at you."

She rolled her eyes. "Seriously, Luc. Guys don't think of me like that."

"Yes, they do," he said, sounding oddly sure about it as he took her hand and helped her out of the booth, leading her outside.

He let go of her hand to put his arm around her and draw her close to him, and she luxuriated in the warmth of his body in the cool night air.

She heard male voices and realized the group from the diner was following them.

Had Luc been right to be paranoid?

Luc's face was stern, but he kept his pace calm, his energy reserved. They were nearly to the car when she felt a hand on her arm, jerking her away from him. She was shoved against the side of the car and turned to see a large man in a leather jacket looking down at her.

Two others were in front of Luc, blocking his way to her. "Wallet," the guy demanded, holding out his palm.

Luc shook his head. "No. Get out of here." He looked over at her to make sure she was okay.

She bit her lip and looked at Luc. Why was he resisting? "Luc…"

The guy in front of her reached out to touch her face, and she flinched back just as he went flying out from in front of her. Luc was there, almost as if he'd teleported, and the guys who'd been blocking him a moment ago seemed confused.

"How'd he do that?" one muttered.

"So fast," the other said.

Luc folded his arms. Hallie could feel his rigid strength in front of her and knew he wasn't going to let anything happen.

* * *

"I wouldn't try that again if I were you," Luc said darkly, trying to maintain his cool but seething with rage.

For too long, Luc had to hear the grotesque thoughts these men had been sharing, the unspeakable things they had casually considered about the woman he was feeling more protective of every minute.

And to top it off, they had come out here and were now attempting to steal from them like common robbers.

Sometimes humans really were the worst.

For a moment, the man he'd stepped in front of flinched at Luc's size. But then, emboldened by his buddies coming up to join him, he took a step forward.

"Threats, huh?" he said with a smirk. "Maybe we oughta teach this guy to be more polite."

"Yeah, and to share his girl," another said from behind.

That was *it*.

Instantly, Luc grabbed the man in front of him by the collar and jerked him up in the air, letting him dangle like a rag doll. He sent a vicious glare at his buddies who were now trying to back up as their leader struggled in his grip.

Then he took a step forward, aimed, and launched the man at them, sending him flying through the air and knocking the others over as they grunted from the impact.

Humans like this didn't threaten him at all. All they threatened was a world where he could protect humans, bond with humans, trust humans.

And he hated them for it.

"Bastards. You'll regret ever even *thinking* about her like that," he said, his voice chilling, his breath getting colder and icier with each passing second.

Without hesitation, he strode forward to the men

as they scrambled to get up off the ground. He kicked hard into one man's gut, so hard the man slid backward and rammed into a nearby brick wall, knocking him unconscious.

Seeing the imminent danger, the remaining guys clambered to their feet. Upon getting up, one tried to retaliate, swinging a wild fist at Luc, but he just side-stepped effortlessly, the punch almost slow motion compared to his reflexes.

He then countered with a jab across the man's face, the force of it throwing him to the side as a crunch resounded off the nearby cars and building in the parking lot, the sound of it not the least unsatisfying.

He was losing himself again; he could feel it. But he wanted to punish them, both for what they had tried to do and what they'd been picturing in their minds.

But as he fought, he could sense Hallie watching, could sense her worry and fear, and that pulled him back slightly from the icy mental ledge he was dangling over.

By now, the last man had risen to his feet and was reaching behind him to pull out something. Luc whirled around and grabbed the man's hand, which was gripping a gun.

For a second, Luc just stared at the weapon, leaving it pointed skyward. Then in one quick motion, he ripped it free from the man's grasp and crushed it in his grip like a soda can, letting the pieces clatter to the ground.

When the ringleader saw he was clearly outmatched and his lackeys were incapacitated, he showed his true colors, jerking his hand free and trying to run for the street. But Luc snagged him by his leather jacket and hauled him off the ground, holding him by the neck as the man struggled fruitlessly against his unwavering dragon strength.

Luc could sense the coldness in him growing colder. Could see himself unleashing his dragon breath on the thug, freezing him solid so he couldn't hurt anyone again.

But he could also feel another part to him, one that was slowly waking up, telling him to let go.

It was hard, though. The strength of his restraining collar was weakened when a human was in danger, giving him access to more of his power. It was hard to contain all of that iciness.

By now, the man's face was turning red as he tried to claw and kick and free himself from Luc's grasp. Finally, he calmed the raging beast inside him long enough to toss the man away to a nearby dumpster. With enough force to make him think twice about his life of crime, but certainly not enough to end him.

He turned back Hallie, still watching in amazement, and felt warmth coursing through him again. She was safe; that was all that mattered.

This time, he hadn't lost everything.

He walked to her and put his arms around her, sinking into her embrace for just a second. She hugged him back, giving comfort, but then he pulled back, realizing they needed to get out of there before anyone else came along.

"I'm sorry for all that. Let's get you back home," he said.

Her eyes were still wide with shock as he guided her toward her door. "I mean, but what just happened?

The gun, and you..." She shook her head. "That was amazing, but I'm so confused."

"Later," he said as he helped her in, then came back around to his door.

But as he did, he saw the ringleader charging toward him one last time, a knife in his hand.

Dammit, why did humans make it impossible to show mercy?

Instantly, the dragon inside him kicked into action, and he felt power surge through him as he focused on the attacker and breathed.

The man immediately froze in place, knife in hand, his body still as a statue, cold as ice.

Luc walked close to the man, hearing his shallow breaths as he tried to move but was unable to.

"You're lucky she's here, or I would have frozen you until every cell in your body exploded." He made sure the man could hear him, while Hallie could not.

Then Luc turned, got in the car, and drove off, leaving the frozen man with time to thaw and reconsider his life choices.

CHAPTER 7

Hallie couldn't believe what she'd just seen.

Luc. Quiet, mild-mannered Luc, who sometimes seemed he was from a different planet, tossing three men all over the place.

It was like he was bowling with human bodies.

He'd crushed a gun as if it were made of Styrofoam. Suddenly, he wasn't just odd because of his weird social habits and manner of speaking.

Now he seemed almost alien. Especially the way he'd made that last guy go completely still. It was otherworldly.

She and Luc definitely needed to have a talk.

Still, he'd defended her. That gave her a warm,

contented feeling. Like no matter what was weird about him, she was safe. Like she wasn't wrong to trust him.

The drive was quiet, because she could sense he needed to calm down. She did as well.

When they pulled up in front of her small house in her small, quiet neighborhood, she got out the same time he did and came around. He put his arm out again, and she took it, leading him up the front steps.

"Want to come in?" she asked.

He nodded silently. In the light of her porch, his blond hair was mussed, there were lines around his eyes, and he didn't look at all ready to leave her.

She turned on the lights as she showed him into her home. They walked into her modestly furnished but clean living room, and she gestured for him to take the biggest couch. He did and then just stared at her, looking more than ever like a huge, confused alien in human form.

"We have to talk about what just happened," she said. "There's no way I can just believe you're normal."

He shrugged. "Think what you want."

"Do you mean that?" she asked, irritated. She

folded her arms. "Are you seriously going to pretend I didn't see what I just saw?"

He looked up at her, heat in his blue eyes. "I protected you. That's all that should matter. And I'll do it again and again if I have to. I'll see it as a privilege."

"But..." She fought back a blush. "I mean, I'm grateful you protected us. But you... the gun... the guys..."

"What about them?" he asked stubbornly.

She came over to join him on the couch. "Humans don't crush guns with their bare hands or knock people over like bowling pins."

"Was that like bowling?" he asked flatly, leaning back in the chair. "If so, I kind of liked it."

"I didn't," she said. "We were in danger."

"I didn't like that part," he said. "What I liked was the way they flew away from you. The way I could protect you and keep them from touching you. Punish them for thinking bout you."

"There you go again," she said with a sigh, giving him a rueful smile. "Look, humans just don't talk like that. Because we don't read minds."

"Maybe some do," he said.

"Do they also freeze people in place?" she asked. "Seriously, Luc, I like you. I'm starting to *really* like you. But I need more of the truth from you if we're going to get any closer."

He was quiet a long moment, studying his hands as he slowly rubbed the palms together. Such long, deft, powerful fingers.

She'd always known he was probably too good to be true, but she had no idea what he was.

"If I'm not human, what do you think I am?" he asked.

"Well, if you hadn't beat those men up, I'd say some kind of angel," she said. "Just looking at you, I mean."

"Angel?" he asked.

"You know, sent from heaven. Wings?"

He laughed hoarsely. "I may have wings. But I'm *no* angel."

A shiver went through her. "Then what are you?"

He just stared at her more, not offering any answers. She couldn't even believe she was having this conversation. She'd never thought about the existence of other beings in this world.

But as he stared at her, looking perfectly relaxed with those glowing blue eyes, she knew she was looking at one now.

But she had no idea what he was.

"You have wings, but you're no angel," she said. "Vampire?"

"No," he said, a small smile quirking his lips. "I don't suck blood."

"A superhero?" she asked. "From another planet?"

"No," he said.

"I give up," she said.

"Is it enough to just know I'm different, but I would never hurt you?" he asked, leaning in to stroke one hand over her cheek.

Warmth filled her, taking away all her anxiety, and she sank into it

What did it matter what he was when she felt this good around him? She'd never seen him do anything but good things, except when evil people needed to be taught a lesson.

Then he was downright scary.

But this Luc was another Luc altogether. Kind. Warm. Soothing. Like the iciness that was usually around him pulled back just a little, letting her see the true him inside.

"All right," she said. "I'll stop the third degree for now. Whatever you are, thank you for saving me," she said, leaning against his shoulder. He tightened up and then relaxed, bringing his hand around her. Even after the violence he'd wrought, being here touching him felt completely right.

"I mean, I'll try not to think about it, but how did you do that?" she asked, mostly babbling to herself. "How did you make that man freeze like that, and how did you—"

She was cut off as his lips closed over hers, his hands burying themselves in her hair, his breath mingling with hers as they kissed deeply.

He drew back, keeping their foreheads together, his eyes averted downward.

"What would you say if I told you I was a

monster?" he asked, sounding desperate beneath the calm tone of his voice. "What if I told you I wasn't good?"

She looked into his eyes, unfathomable, swirling blue. "I would try to understand why you felt that so I could tell you you were wrong."

He was quiet for a moment, his thumb stroking gently over her temple. "I wish I was an angel, for you."

She smiled softly, enjoying his touch. "Whatever you are is enough for me." She put her hand over his. "Let's just enjoy what we have."

The woman inside her didn't want to waste another second. If he truly was something from another world, she didn't know how much time she had with him. And even if she would have said this was crazy only a few days ago, right now, the only thing that felt crazy was not taking the chance she'd been given.

She reached a hand around his neck. "Can you read my mind?"

"I could, but I don't want to."

"Why?" she asked, already breathless just from

his stare.

He drew a finger over her ear and down her neck. "Because I can usually tell what you're thinking. And anything else, I would want you to tell me on your own. I don't want to steal anything."

She was touched by that, felt warmth pooling in her belly like hot chocolate. She moved in until their lips were super close again, letting the tension tingle between them.

He closed the distance, his hand snaking around her back and pulling her in tight against him, his kiss becoming urgent, possessive, as his lips left her mouth and travelled over her neck, to her collarbone, over the tops of her breasts where they met. Up to her shoulders. Kissing and caressing and making his mark all over her skin. Searing her to the core.

"Luc," she gasped. "Don't stop."

"I couldn't," he said, picking her up in his arms. "Not with all the magic powers in the world." He looked around. "Where is your room?"

She pointed to the stairs, and he stormed toward them. Apparently, he felt all the heat and urgency she did. That whatever was between them was something wonderful that needed to be explored right freaking now.

A taut sexual tension she'd been feeling since they first met. Judging by his possessive hands on her, the feelings were mutual.

When he reached her door, he kicked it open, making it bang against the wall on the other side.

"You didn't have to do that," she said, gasping as he tossed her on her bed and then crawled over her with a growl.

He was so big, so feral.

Maybe she'd been thinking wrong when she'd thought of him as a human shape of an angel or superhero. Maybe she needed to think more along the lines of *animal*.

"This is crazy," she said as he entwined his hands over hers and pinned her back against the mattress.

He nodded, blue eyes cool as he awaited her permission. She struggled slightly against his hands and grinned. She wasn't feeling any pain. Her meds must still be working.

It was time for her body to feel more than just pain or the absence of it. She wanted to feel everything. With Luc.

"Are you okay?" he asked in a low voice.

"More than okay," she said, looking up at him boldly. "Take me."

CHAPTER 8

A dangerous cocktail of emotions whirled inside Luc as he looked down on Hallie, this beautiful, angelic person that made him question everything he believed about humans and existence itself.

Yet when she smiled, everything melted away, the clouds departed, and he could feel warmth again. Happiness, even if just a small sliver warming his ice-cold blood.

Keeping her hands pinned above her, he came down for another kiss. This time it was hot, erotic. She struggled lightly against his iron grip, and then she relaxed more deeply into the kiss, melting beneath him like spring snow before the rising sun.

His tongue teased at the entrance to her mouth, and she opened, letting him lick and stroke inside her. Her muffled moans only made him dive deeper, exploring her until he knew every sensitive spot, every tiny flick that would make her body move underneath him.

When he finally left her mouth, she gave out a long, pleasured sigh, as if this were a new experience to her.

Instantly, the thought of another man touching her like this made him want to do it a thousand times more to completely eradicate her memory of anything but his kiss.

Possessively, he moved to her earlobe, still pinning her with his hands as he moved his body closer to hers, close enough that their bodies brushed, his skin warming even at the slightest touch even though they still had their clothes between them. Hallie squeaked softly with delight as he kissed, then licked, then bit down lightly on her soft skin, intensifying the pressure further and further to increase her arousal.

But the more her body reacted to him, the more

he wanted her, *needed* her to feel more. More pleasure. More desire. More arousal.

He freed her hands long enough to help her out of her dress and bra, leaving her with just her underwear, and immediately he went to work on the pleasantly warm, indescribably soft breasts. While his right hand kneaded and rubbed her nipple with his thumb, his mouth licked and suckled on the other. And each touch, each lick was amply rewarded by her body's response, letting him know just how much she felt.

"Don't stop," she pleaded, writhing beneath him, struggling against his grip yet overwhelmed by the things he did, unable to escape the pleasure he wanted to give in never-ending quantities.

His tongue explored lower on her body, kissing everywhere on her belly and finding her belly button as his hand felt along the curve of her hips, then her waist, moving lower and lower toward the center of her pleasure. Luc found himself torn between wanting to let the buildup of tension in her body finally free or pushing her to the very limits of her control, drawing out the wait until she could take it no more.

But with each moan, each quiver of pleasure, Luc found it harder to keep control himself.

She'd thought he was an angel. That was preposterous.

But angel or demon, he would protect her. Would keep her safe and keep her his, no matter what stood against him.

He kissed a small trail along the line of her panties, making her gasp with anticipation. Then his finger found her center, caressing over the soft fabric of her underwear as she squirmed with pleasure.

That was absolutely delightful.

He continued to stroke up the center of her hips, making sure his fingers found the small nub that made her tremble more and more with heated arousal. And as he did, he held her down, witnessing every movement she made, every tiny gasp of air or elongated moan of want, as she came closer and closer to the brink.

Finally, Luc felt her come beneath him, her back arching as she cried out in ecstasy. He continued to hold Hallie, watching with captivation as she rode out the intense release that washed over her.

There really was nothing else like it in the universe, seeing his special woman experience overwhelming pleasure that *he* had given her.

Even as she slowly relaxed under his grip, the incredible sight of seeing her come only made him more insatiable, a kind of lust that could never be slaked.

He finally let go of her arms, and she let them relax above her on the pillow as he carefully removed her panties, leaving her entirely bare and amazingly beautiful. And as he spread her legs, he saw her go wide-eyed with captivation as he lowered himself over her, her floral scent as intoxicating as her touch.

He licked once against her clit, slow and languorous, savoring every moment of this experience with Hallie as she writhed with intense satisfaction. When her hands grasped the bed sheets, as if searching, begging for something to hold on to, he reached toward them and grasped them with his own, holding her down once again as he pleasured her thoroughly.

And the more he did, the more he could hear the feral dragon inside him rumbling. *Mate*, it demanded.

But Luc pushed it away as he focused on Hallie, focused on the way her hips bucked if he went too fast. Focused on the way she turned her head to the side and moaned when he made little circles with his tongue around her clit. Focused on every curve of her body, every blush or twitch or movement she made in response to his onslaught of pleasure.

He continued to explore, running his tongue lower and thrusting into her, her heat and wetness as erotic as it was bewitching. He could almost feel what it would be like to be inside her, be one with her. And he could tell she was thinking the same thing just by the satisfied moan she gave out.

Then, with one last, tiny flick of the tip of his tongue on her clit, she came again, even harder this time. But instead of holding her down, he released her hands, allowing her body to do whatever it wanted. Instinctively, she grasped onto him, her nails digging into his shoulders and her legs wrapping around his waist as she cried out his name in release.

As she did, his hands caressed up her thighs as he watched attentively, and she held on to him tightly as every last drop of pleasure was wrung from her, enjoying the feel of her skin as her body rocked with the throes of release.

And as she finally started to relax, Luc considered his next move. By now, her body responded to him more acutely with each touch.

Desire surged through him to take her, right here and right now. To make their bodies come together as one. To experience what he could only imagine would be pure ecstasy for both of them.

But even though Luc was fairly certain he could keep control of his dragon, he honestly had no clue how mating for dragons from his age worked. And the last thing Hallie deserved after all the unfairness in her life was a decision neither of them was ready to make.

"What's wrong?" she asked, aware of his hesitation even through the haze of euphoria she was still coming down from.

"I don't want to stop, but I think we should. I'm not sure what will happen if we go all the way," Luc replied, the dragon inside him rebelling at the thought of stopping, but his mind resolute as to what should be done.

Thankfully, Hallie didn't question it, but looked back at him with contentment and gratitude.

But to his surprise, as he sat up to get off the bed, he felt her hands working on the zipper of his pants with surprising deftness.

"Just because we don't go all the way doesn't mean I don't want one last thing." Her voice was husky as she loosened his belt and pulled his hard member free from the pants he wore.

For a moment, Luc didn't know how to respond as she sat up and kneeled on the bed in front of him. And when she began to run her soft hands along his length, he found himself unaware of what to do now that he was no longer the one in control.

She was, and she knew it, sending him a knowing little grin as she stroked him.

The little minx.

To start, Hallie moved slowly, as if savoring the feel of him as he'd savored the taste of her only a moment ago.

"You feel amazing," she said, grasping him

tighter and making him nearly lose it at the sight of her pleasure. "Why can't we go all the way?"

She sounded slightly disappointed, so he put his own hands to work, cupping her full breasts and massaging them as she stroked harder and harder along him.

"I just don't know," he said. "I want to be careful with you. Go slow."

"Giving me that many orgasms is going slow?" she murmured.

"As slow as I can go," he grated out.

As she intensified the pleasure, he did, too, pressing his fingers against her nipples as he dipped his head to kiss the base of her neck.

And despite his ample control, his entire body felt like fire, white heat building inside him as she moved quicker. He allowed himself to at least think about being inside her, the image of their two bodies coming together vivid as he felt himself get harder and harder beneath her touch.

Luc brought his finger down between Hallie's legs as she eagerly touched him with fevered speed.

Then with a single flick of her clit, she came one last time, her grip tightening and seizing the very last inch of his will past its ability to resist her embrace.

Together they came, arms wrapped around each other, his entire body alight with all-consuming fire that wrenched its release through him over and over.

For a very long—impossibly long—moment, they stayed together, Hallie's face nestled on his chest while he kept his arms around her, holding her, not wanting to let go, both of them saying nothing, their heaving breaths the only sound in the room.

Nobody had ever made him feel like this. So wanted. So needed.

And he could barely comprehend his own need for Hallie. So great it was, as vital as air itself.

But even lying there after the greatest pleasure of his life, something was bothering him. The strong urge to be with her, to claim her, felt almost as desperate as his need for oxygen.

The necklace felt like it was strangling him. Just one claiming with her and he'd be free to heal her. Free to be himself again, whoever that was.

Free to own her forever.

But he didn't even know what that entailed. Hadn't thought to ask before because it hadn't seemed possible he would find a human mate.

But after sharing this with Hallie, he knew for sure she was it. He just didn't know where to go from here, and he didn't want to fuck things up.

He ran his hand absentmindedly over her hair as he tried to calm the dragon pacing inside him.

Mate. Mate. Mate. Like a heartbeat.

It should be enough to just be with her like he had been, and he didn't want to leave her. But having her curvy body against him, so precious and warm, the feelings of need weren't leaving him.

Perhaps he needed to cool off before he did something they'd both regret. As much as he wanted her, it would be unfair to mate her before she even knew what he was.

He sat up, removing his arm from her reluctantly as she faced him, her skin glowing, her soft, gray eyes loving.

"I need to go," he said.

Her face fell just a fraction and then went back to her normal calm. She nodded, pulling the sheet around her as he got out of bed and began doing up his pants.

She stared at him, and he could sense the awkwardness between them. "Did I do something?" she said.

He looked at her. "No, of course not."

"Then why are you leaving?"

He cocked his head. He didn't have an acceptable answer for that, so he just shrugged. Hopefully, if he just made it look casual, it wouldn't be a big deal between them and they could start over fresh tomorrow at work.

"A shrug? Really?" She looked exasperated.

She was getting angrier. It was time to go. "I'll go out the window," he said. "I have everything with me, and then you don't have to get up and lock the door, okay?" She was still undressed, and he didn't want to bother her.

She simply raised an eyebrow as he went to the window. When he made sure she was covered, he opened it and squeezed himself through, dropping to the pavement with a thud that barely bothered him.

With longing, he looked back up at the window, but she wasn't there.

It had been an amazing date. He'd made more progress than he'd ever thought. But it was time to go see Zach.

CHAPTER 9

Luc was beginning to think it had been a mistake to leave after making love with Hallie, but he hadn't known what to do.

He'd gone straight to Zach the night before, so he could explain what he knew about mating, both how to do it and the effects thereof. Apparently, he needed to give her the ring he'd been given at birth, which had powers that would protect her as his mate.

Luc only knew the ring was an heirloom; it had never occurred to him that some of his powers might be bound up within it. But if it protected Hallie, he wanted her to have it.

Once she knew who and what he was.

The thing was telling her that was scary. Almost as scary as hoping for something when that hope could go awry.

What if something happened? There was too much he couldn't control in this world. But he also knew he couldn't stay away from her. Or Bastien. Too much was riding on it.

He was getting ready to get into the Volvo to drive himself to the shelter when Zach came out of the house to talk to him, hands shoved in his pockets.

"You doing okay?" he asked.

"Yeah," Luc answered.

"Okay. Just checking." Zach looked to the side. "You coming back tonight?"

"I don't know," Luc said. "Should I not?"

Zach leaned on the car for a moment, letting the breeze ruffle his long, dark hair. "I think you should consider it. Look, I don't know what changed you all those years ago, but I do know you're finally starting to act like your old self. And if I were you, I'd try to hold on to whatever was making me do that."

Luc nodded. "I know that much. I'm just not sure

it's fair to her."

"Why?" Zach asked. "You're the most squeaky clean of the dragons. She's lucky to get someone as uncomplicated as you."

"What if I'm not uncomplicated?" Luc asked, not wanting to tell even his friend what had happened. "What if I have serious issues?"

"Then maybe you should tell someone and let it out, rather than letting it kill you inside or keep you from happiness."

"It's not killing me," Luc muttered, folding his arms. "But it does bother me that I'm not who you think I am. Not who the oracle thinks I am. Not who Hallie thinks I am."

"Just because we don't agree with your own assessment of yourself doesn't mean we're wrong," Zach said stubbornly, patting the car door as it shut.

Luc rolled down the window. "I don't know if I'll be home tonight, but I'll let you know."

"Aw, sweet," Zach teased.

Luc sent him a scowl that probably only amused him and then pulled out of the driveway.

Driving was getting easier, and he allowed himself to actually relax into the chair and pull sunglasses on as he pulled onto the freeway.

Music was playing on the radio, and with the sun shining outside, he truly felt like maybe he was starting to become a part of this world.

A part of him worried he was just convincing himself things were fine, just like he'd tried to convince himself and the other dragons back in the day that it was okay for dragons to intervene.

But it was different this time. There were no little, vulnerable villages and no marauders, and he could protect the people he cared about with his own two hands.

He pulled up in front of the shelter and took a deep breath. Hallie was in there, and hopefully, she wouldn't be hiding that disappointed look like she had when he'd left.

He hadn't gone because he didn't want to stay with her. He'd left because it was all so fast and confusing. And because he didn't want to make a wrong move

He'd been carefree and ambitious in his other life, and this time, he was trying to be careful, for everyone's sake. Or maybe mostly for the sake of his own heart.

He locked the car and went in, noticing it was a little busier than usual.

Hallie was in front of the desk, talking to a family about adoption, so Luc decided not to bother her. Instead, he took a look at the outfit she was wearing, black leggings with a pink pullover tee shirt and black flats. He smiled in approval and headed back to clean cages and see Bastien.

He noticed the little cat pop its head up the minute he entered. Despite the work he had to do, he would let himself just see how Bastien was doing.

He unlocked the cage and took the cat out, examining his leg. It wasn't better, but it wasn't worse, and from what Hallie had said, that was the best that could be expected. He stroked the cat, enjoying his calming purr, and felt a prickle of unease over his neck as the door opened.

He looked over his shoulder and saw Hallie

coming in with a man he didn't recognize.

He narrowed his eyes, scenting the air. The other man was tall, large enough he could be a shifter, but carrying no scent that would indicate he was one.

Hm.

He had reddish-orange hair, a slightly smushed-looking face, and was overweight.

Or maybe he was just a really large human. An untrustworthy one. Now that some of his empathy and instincts were coming back, he was remembering just how sharply he could judge people. That would come in handy while protecting his mate.

Shit. Mate. He was thinking it so casually now. So openly.

He saw the man grin creepily from across the room, his hand raised and ready to land on Hallie's shoulder just before she stepped forward, out of reach.

Luc let out a little sigh of relief and set Bastien back in the cage, locking it behind him. "Sorry, little guy. Can't play long today." Then he straightened and grabbed the cleaning supplies so he could work while still keeping an eye on Hallie.

It was awkward between them; he could already tell. She caught him staring, and there was a slight glare on her face when they made eye contact.

He sighed. He'd have to explain everything later. She would just have to trust him for now. He'd never expected everything to go like this, and he was learning as he went.

Still, he didn't like the guy next to her, and he didn't know how much longer he could wait before letting her know.

"So you were saying a puppy?" she asked, looking down the rows. "Did you have a breed in mind?"

"No," he said, following her a little too closely. Luc glared at him, but the man ignored him as they crossed to the other side of the room. "Do you have a boyfriend?"

Hallie turned to him in shock, her gray eyes wide. Her dark hair was pulled into a ponytail that laid over her shoulder, soft and tantalizing. Then again, every part of her was tantalizing.

He tried to read the other man's thoughts but

didn't hear anything. That was odd.

"Um, that doesn't have anything to do with adoption," she said, sending Luc a worried look like she thought he might pop off and cause trouble.

He could, but he wouldn't. He'd already learned the other night that he could hold off his dragon for her.

Still, the guy better watch it.

"So, Bill, do any of these dogs look like what you're looking for?" she asked.

The man finally stopped ogling Hallie long enough to look at the cages in a bored motion.

A thought from the creep finally came into Luc's mind. The man didn't really want to adopt a puppy. But he would enjoy hurting one.

Luc stood abruptly. "You're not adopting," he snapped furiously, walking over to stand between Hallie and the pets and the red-haired jerk.

The man just folded his arms over his massive belly and sneered. "You're just a volunteer. I think it's up to the employees to make that call."

"I..." Hallie looked between them. Then she sighed and took Luc by the arm, hauling him into a corner and lowering her voice to a whisper. "What are you doing? You know we need every adoption we can get."

Luc shook his head. "Not that one. Trust me."

"What is it?" she asked.

Luc didn't know if he wanted to tell her. The thought that someone would hurt animals was a gross one, and he wished he could get the man's nasty thoughts out of his head. So why share it with her?

"I just don't like him," he said.

"Luc..." She sighed. "You don't have a right to get jealous when we don't even know what this is."

"What what is?" he asked, perplexed.

She gestured between them with her hands. "This. You know? We work together, and I've only just met you, and yes, we went out on a date..."

"We did more than that," he said tersely, looking over to make sure the other man wasn't watching. "I think we did enough that you should be able to take my word for it when I say someone is a creep."

"Is he a creep, or are you just jealous?" she asked. "Because so far, I don't have any reason not to trust

Bill. He has been a donor a long time."

Luc's mouth twisted. "So you're going to trust him over me?"

"What choice do I have?" she asked, folding her arms. "You aren't giving me any information."

"Should I have to tell you exactly why every time I don't want you around a man?"

She shook her head. "You aren't my boyfriend, as far as I know, so you don't get to tell me when you do or don't want me around a man. Last night was fun, Luc. But it doesn't give you the right to control me."

Luc frowned. Something was wrong with the whole situation. She wasn't being her usually bright, sunny self. She was defensive toward him. "Is this because I left last night?"

She flipped her hair. "Because you left? How about because the second we finished, you literally jumped out the window? That was a big deal for me, and you didn't say anything. You didn't—"

He leaned in for a kiss, but she pushed him back. "No," she said. "You can't solve this one like this. You can't just kiss a problem away." She looked around him. "Besides, I'm at work."

"What is it you want?" he asked. "I feel like I've done something wrong, and I have no idea what it is."

"Look, Luc, I really like you. But you need to decide what you want. What we are. Because I can't do things like we did last night and watch you disappear through the window. I need someone who is going to stay."

He blinked, too stupefied by what she'd said to notice she was walking back to Bill, the douchebag. Then he did notice.

She was talking to him again, and she saw Bill reach up to put his hand on her arm. She drew back politely, and Luc slumped on a bench, looking at Bastien.

Bastien raised his head, looked in Bill's direction, and hissed, and Luc grinned.

"I'm with you, buddy. He's gotta go."

CHAPTER 10

Hallie was discussing adoptions with Bill in the front waiting room when the door opened with a clang.

Luc strode through, and she put a hand to her forehead as she realized he was coming straight for Bill, who was currently holding an adoption application.

"Do you do home studies?" he asked, giving her a look with his dull green eyes that he seemed to think was flirtatious. "I'd love to have you over. Tell me if my place is right for a dog."

She frowned. "I mean, we don't typically, but—"

"I told you you weren't adopting," Luc roared, and Hallie gasped as the man was hauled off his feet and literally dragged to the door and tossed out on the sidewalk.

They all watched as Bill clambered to his feet, fuming, stormed away from the shelter, and got in his expensive car, driving away without a word.

It had all happened in seconds, and the waiting room was dead silent.

Luc let out an angry breath, staring at the place where the man had been, and then turned on his heel and paced back in with the cages as if nothing had happened.

Oh, no you don't.

She chased after him, giving a look to the other workers that told them to get things moving again, to make people forget the scene that had just taken place.

"What was that about?" she snapped, when she found him standing in front of Bastien's cage.

Luc looked over his shoulder, his blue eyes cold. "I told you he shouldn't adopt."

"And I told you that wasn't your call."

"Can you read minds?" he asked arrogantly, standing at his full, intimidating height. It was odd to see him cocky, because usually he was so quiet.

"Maybe if you can, you can tell me what you saw in him that made you want to let him take an animal."

She sighed in frustration, clenching her hands into fists. "Of course I can't see into everyone's minds. There is always a reason to judge people, but I need every adoption I can get. Many people aren't perfect yet can still take care of a pet."

"So that's it. You think I threw him out because he's not perfect?"

"I think it's because you're jealous," she said, marching over to him. "And I'm beginning to think you're impulsive. Do you think about what you do, or just do it?"

"When I know it's right, I just do it," he said, his voice a low growl. "I don't know why you're harassing me instead of thanking me for throwing out that creep."

"Thanks to you, I have to call and apologize," she said. "And hope he doesn't sue us."

Luc looked a little stymied at that but shook his head. "He shouldn't be anywhere near this place. Trust me on that."

She threw up her hands. "I want to trust you, Luc.

I really do. But you don't tell me anything. You make love to me and... ugh!"

He took her by the arms and turned her toward him. "So this is what it's really about. You're mad I left."

"I'm mad you just walk in here like nothing happened. I'm mad that I feel used. I'm mad that you didn't even text to say you got home. You don't just get to make love to a woman and hop out the window!" Her chest heaved, and she tossed her hair again, looking like an angry, glorious Amazon.

But her words struck him. "We didn't make love. All the way."

Her face went stormy, her gray eyes darkening to the color of rainclouds. "Oh. I see. You stopped it midway so you wouldn't have to feel guilty." She started to stride away, but he caught her gently around the waist, pulling her against him.

"Wait," he said, feeling her body respond to his heat.

She shook him off, and he let her go, astonished. "No, Luc. You're so damn persuasive. And sexy. I get that. But I need more than that. I can't have someone so volatile around. You can't just throw people!"

"So is this about throwing people or about you feeling rejected because I didn't sleep over?"

There was a sneer in his voice, and it made her want to throw dog bones at his stupid head.

She was a patient person. She tried to give people a lot of leeway. But yes, if she put aside everything else, she was hurt. She'd been hurt the moment he'd left, because she'd been looking forward to somebody holding her for the first time in a long time.

And he'd gotten what he'd wanted and just left.

"You didn't look mad when I said I needed to go," he said, frowning. "I didn't think you'd mind."

"I didn't want you to stay if you didn't want to," she said.

"Then I don't see what the problem is."

She curled her hands into fists again. A wave of pain went through her. "I don't have time for this. I need my meds. And you need to go home and think about how to be more professional."

He narrowed his eyes as he put away the cleaning

supplies, shaking his head. "I just don't get what you want from me."

She gritted her teeth together, feeling like she shouldn't have to explain. Did she really seem like the type of girl that would do that with a guy she didn't care about? Someone she just wanted to kick out after?

But for him, it must have been casual. Disposable. She'd been dumb for thinking this was a fairy tale and not another guy using her.

Ugh, she hated she'd been dumb enough to get swept off her feet.

"If you didn't want me to go, you should have said so," he said, walking past her, a look of frustration on his face.

"If you didn't want to stay, why would I make you?" she retorted, turning her back as he exited.

She heard his footsteps pause at the door and glared over at him.

"Can we talk later?" he asked, hesitant. Damn, he was so handsome he took her breath away. And he really didn't seem to know what was going on. But did that make it okay to just toy with her feelings?

She tapped her foot a few times. "Not tonight, okay? I need some rest." She put a hand on her back. "And some meds."

He opened his mouth as if to offer something but then shut it. Which was good. She didn't want him trying to do anything nice right now.

"You aren't really going to call that guy, are you?" he asked.

She sighed. "Thanks to you, I have to."

"What do you mean thanks to me?"

"Look. You may be from another planet, but I live on this one. And we need money. Donations. And not to be sued. And when someone physically hurts another person, there are consequences."

"Well, if you had listened to me, I wouldn't have had to throw him out."

"And violence is always the answer for you, is that it?" she asked.

His eyes went deadly cold, and he turned away from her, silent.

"Look, this is just... We're both tired. Clearly, we both need space. And you don't need to worry about my work. I'll handle it, as I always have."

He said nothing, just walked out the door and let it shut behind him with a loud, resounding clang.

She sat on a bench and looked over at Bastien. "Dammit, what should I do?"

Bastien didn't say anything. Just curled in a little ball and looked over at the door like he missed Luc.

She did, too.

* * *

Luc paced the living room, anger unfurling in him as he stomped angrily over the now frozen carpet.

"Can you stop that?" Erin asked, leaning back in her chair and watching with mild annoyance. "Zach, make him stop."

Zach was perched next to her and shook his head. "I don't know if I can. Sapphire is strong."

"Ha!" Luc let out a bitter bark. "Strong. Strong is useless with women."

"What happened?" Erin said. "If you just calm down and tell us, maybe we can help."

"There are evil people all over this fucking planet; that's the problem," Luc said. "And my human won't listen to me and gets mad at me when I protect her. That's the other problem." He pulled at his hair. "I mean, how am I supposed to do this if she won't even listen?"

"Hallie has always seemed like a reasonable woman to me," Erin said thoughtfully. "So I don't know what you mean."

"There was a guy at the shelter today. A complete creep. Coming on to her, touching her." He ran his hand through his hair, messing it up further, knowing he looked ridiculous, but not caring as long as he and Hallie were fighting. "And he wanted to adopt. But he was thinking about hurting puppies." He glared at nothing in particular. "How evil can you get?"

"Wait, so is this about the puppies, or is this about the guy hitting on Hallie?" Zach asked.

"Both. I don't know," Luc said, waving a hand. "What it's about is she doesn't trust me. She's angry with me, and I have no idea why."

"What happened on your date?" Erin asked. "I don't know a lot of details, but Zach said it went well."

Luc shook his head. Should he share that with

her?

"Go ahead," Zach said. "I'm okay with it."

"It went well, I think," Luc said. "I mean, I got in a fight to protect her and showed her some things I can't really explain, but I felt like she accepted me for me. And we... did stuff. Good stuff. I mean, I care about her. But I don't know what mating entails and didn't want to screw up, so I left."

"Oh," Erin said.

"And she said it was fine," Luc said, whirling on his heel. "I mean, she looked slightly disappointed, but—"

"Wait, you slept with her and then left immediately after?" Erin asked.

"You didn't tell me that," Zach said, putting a hand over his face. "Dude, not cool."

Luc raised an eyebrow. "What was the problem? She was a temptation, and I needed to get far enough away that I could think things over. And plus, I knew we would be seeing each other the next morning. Why should one night matter?"

"Because you'd just been intimate," Erin said,

looking aggravated. "And to a girl, that really means something."

"It means something to me, too," Luc said. "It means I care enough to be careful and not lock her into something she didn't want."

"Have you explained that to her?"

"No," Luc said. "I thought she would trust me."

"Doesn't sound very trustworthy to me," Erin said. "I mean, you've been trying to spend all the time you can with her ever since you met her. You took a job there, for Pete's sake. And then you get her in the sack and just can't run away fast enough? I can see why she doesn't trust you."

When she put it that way, Luc had to admit it sounded bad.

"And then with this guy, she said it wasn't my business because I wasn't her boyfriend. As if I even know what that means." He kept ranting.

"Oh," Erin said. "So that's what she wants."

"Huh?"

"Some girls really want commitment," Erin explained. "I wish the two of you had been more upfront with each other."

"Commitment?" he asked. "I'm committed. Committed as hell. I want to follow her everywhere and make sure no one touches her."

Erin cocked her head. "Well, I guess that kinda means what humans call a boyfriend."

"So I am one, then?" he asked hopefully.

"If you want to be, you'll need to ask her," she said. "I don't know. What happened today when you went in?"

"I sort of... threw the guy out of the shelter because she wouldn't listen, and he was evil and he was touching her..."

"So you're sending really mixed messages," Erin said.

He threw his hands up. "I don't think so. I took her on a date. I kissed her. I protected her. I took space so I could keep her safe even from myself, and I showed up the next morning to see her again. Then I did what I needed to in order to get filth out of her way. All of these are the same message to me," he said stubbornly.

Erin looked at her mate, exasperated. "Zach, can you handle this?"

Zach stood, brushed off his legs, and walked over to Luc so they were face to face.

Then he hauled back and punched Luc through the face, sending him spinning.

When Luc regained his balance, he lunged at Zach, knocking him to the ground.

He heard Erin gasp but just grabbed Zach by the collar, raising a fist.

"That's right. Fight back," Zach snarled. "I'm so sick of your bitching and whining. Fight back and be the person you were. No, be a mix of that person and this one. But stop just bottling it up and exploding. Just for once, fight."

Luc sagged back, letting Zach go. Zach brushed off his hands and crawled out from under him. Then he sat a couple feet away, staring at him.

"Look, I know it's easy to fight evil guys. I get you can just throw people around. But that's not why you're here." Zach poked Luc in the chest. "You're here to fight this. To fight the fear that keeps you running from the kind of life Hallie can offer."

Luc sighed. "I'm more worried about the kind of life *I* can offer."

"So you hate yourself," Zach said. "Well, fight against it. It does no one any good. Square off with what's hurting you and let it go. And move on. And be happy. And now that you know what will and won't mate someone, you don't have to run from your woman."

Luc put his hands over his face. "I don't know what I want. I mean, I know, but I don't think I deserve it."

Zach put a hand on his friend's shoulder. "I wish you would tell me why."

"I can't," Luc choked out, memories flooding him. He'd been a good person once. He could remember a time without guilt, a time without self-hatred.

A time when he wouldn't have been worried about fleeing the bed of a woman he loved just because he feared what he'd do to her.

He let out a low breath. The village. The dying.

Could he really just let it all go?

Not yet.

"But in the meantime, what do I do with Hallie?" he asked, more to Erin than Zach. "How do I make it right?"

She sighed. "I don't really know. I mean, I guess you could go the Zach way and just stalk her until you get what you want. Girls like to be pursued, and after all, she wants to know you want her. Not just for a one-night stand."

"One-night stand?" he asked, confused.

"Think about it, dipshit."

"I did not only want her for one night," Luc said.

"Then go tell her that," Zach said, reaching out a hand to help Luc up. When they got to the door, Zach opened it, and as Luc walked through, he got a boot in the butt, shoving him out. "And don't come back tonight. I'm gonna have sex with my woman."

Before Luc could even screw up his face in disgust, Zach was gone.

That was the onyx dragon for you.

Luc brushed himself off, rose his his full height,

and cracked his knuckles.

He had a mate to stalk in order to prove his love.

CHAPTER 11

By the time she got home from work, Hallie was just overall upset with how the day had gone.

She hadn't been able to reach Bill to apologize, and she had no idea if he was going to sue the shelter, which would be a total disaster for everyone involved.

She also hated she'd gone off on Luc. True, he'd hurt her feelings, but he hadn't meant to, and she could have addressed it better. She could have done everything better, but unfortunately, she, like anyone, had bad days, and there wasn't anything she could do about it.

Other than figure out how to make it right.

There was still light outside when she arrived

home, and when she parked, she got out of her car and just leaned against it for a moment, enjoying the evening glow on the large hedge of bushes in front of her house.

She caught movement out of the corner of her eye and saw a man getting out of a parked car and walking toward her. She relaxed some when she realized it was Bill. Maybe he'd gotten her messages and had come to talk to her.

He'd always seemed like a reasonable, even friendly, person, and she didn't want today to jeopardize their working relationship.

She knew Luc would be offended, but long after he decided to do whatever he wanted, she would still be here, taking care of the shelter. After all, Luc had never made any forever promises. It would be stupid to after knowing each other such a short time.

She sighed and walked toward Bill. She frowned as she saw the look on his face. A bit red, mercurial, his eyes glaring. He backed her up in the direction of her house, and she was in front of her car again.

He folded his arms as he stared down at her, not

appearing as he ever had before. "Do you want to explain what happened today? What your *boyfriend* did?"

"He's not my boyfriend," she muttered. "He's an employee who just happens to really care about the animals, and I don't know what upset him today. He's never like that." She gave him a polite smile. "But I'm really, really sorry, and on behalf of the shelter, I'd love to know if there is anything I could do to make it up to you."

He frowned, and then a dark smile curled the corners of his lips. "What did you have in mind?"

Not whatever he seemed to be thinking. Ugh. Maybe he wasn't so nice after all. "I was thinking maybe a plaque on the wall that commends your donations. Or naming a room after you? Something that acknowledges everything you've done?"

He stalked forward, backing her up to the car until her back hit it. He looked her up and down, making her skin crawl. Why oh why had she chased Luc away?

He was turning out to be right about too many

things. Still, why had none of this happened before?

"Why don't *you* acknowledge everything I've done?" Bill said creepily, curling his lip as he got even closer.

She put up a hand to push him away. "Look, I'm sure we can work something out." She tried to side-step around him, but he trapped her further with his huge bulk. She looked around the street for any sign of help but didn't see anything. "Not like this, though."

She struggled again, pushing on him, as he began to pull her into his arms. "Eek! Stop!" She pulled back, fighting to avoid his lips. "Help!"

The bushes behind them rustled, and she looked up in shock to see Luc standing behind Bill, glaring down at him with ominous rage in his icy eyes.

"Oh, you've done it now," he said, grabbing the other guy by the scruff of the neck.

"I didn't mean it. I didn't mean it," the other guy screeched, groveling as he dangled in Luc's grip.

As usual, Luc looked intimidatingly large and angry, but she saw him take a huge breath in an effort to stay calm. Then he glanced over at her, his eyes noting every detail, trying to see what the other man had done.

He turned back to Bill with fury in his stare, letting his hands tighten as the other man struggled. "You touch her again, you're fucking dead. You get it? Dead. Not able to think about torturing puppies, not able to creep on shelter workers. Because you'll be *dead*."

The man nodded, going slightly red. Luc gave him a look of disgust and dropped him.

As Bill got to his feet and started running away, it looked like it was taking every bit of Luc's self-control not to go after him.

He was tense for a few seconds and then exhaled, letting all the air out of his chest. "Are you okay?"

She stayed against the car for a moment, trying to take everything in. She was glad he was here, but where the hell had he come from? She looked around her. Sure enough, down the street where she wouldn't have seen it before, was his black Volvo.

She put a hand to her face. "Yes, I'm fine."

He walked forward, hands in his pockets. "Sorry I

didn't move sooner. I didn't know what you wanted me to do until you yelled for help." He bit his lip. "And I already got in trouble once today for overstepping my bounds."

"You didn't overstep," she said, letting out a shaky breath. "You were just in time." She looked in Bill's direction, where his car was pulling away. "It just... surprised me. I didn't think he'd do that."

Her heart was racing painfully fast. She looked up at Luc, grateful but confused.

"I know," he said. "Let's get you inside." He walked her in, and she sat in her regular chair, still in shock.

What just happened?

She was still thinking about it when Luc brought her a glass of lemonade from the kitchen. "Thanks," she said, bringing it to her lips for a slow sip. As she calmed, she thought over the situation, and something ridiculous struck her.

"You were hiding. In my bushes," she said.

He nodded seriously. "I was stalking you."

She let out a laugh and then covered her mouth.

"Oh my gosh, why on earth were you doing that?"

"I wanted you to know I wanted you. That you weren't a one-night stand," he said.

She looked him over and noted the little bits of shrubbery stuck to his shirt and pants. "How long were you there?"

"A few hours," he said with a shrug. "The right amount I guess." He cracked his knuckles together. "I had no idea that was going to happen, or I'd be staying in your bushes day and night."

"Or you could stay inside with me," she suggested.

He gave her a small smile. "I'd like that." He walked over and pulled a chair next to her, looking pleased with himself. "I didn't beat the crap out of him; did you notice that?"

"I did," she said. "I was pretty impressed."

"I know," he said. "But seriously, are you okay? Because I also wanted to talk to you about last night, if that's okay with you."

"Sure," she said, her heart pounding nervously.

He went back to his couch and leaned forward,

facing her. As usual, his hair was mussed, and he still looked like the most handsome thing she'd ever seen. "I sent the wrong message last night," he said. "I wasn't trying to say I didn't want to commit. It's just, for what I am, mating is a very big deal. And I've never met a woman I wanted to mate, so I didn't know how it worked. You're tempting, and I didn't want to screw something up."

"Whoa, whoa, whoa," she said. "What do you mean screw things up?"

"Trap you," he said. "Mating is permanent."

She rubbed her temples with both hands. "I don't know what that means, mating. Are you some kind of animal?"

"Not exactly," he said.

"Are you ever going to tell me what you are?" she asked.

"I think so," he said. "When the time is right." He sat up with a long sigh. "Okay, so from the top... When I came here, I was given a mission. One I didn't think I could complete." He touched his necklace. "I was supposed to prove I could care about the human world.

I didn't want to ever do that again. I cared once, and it broke me. It broke a lot of people." Guilt clouded his blue eyes, and he looked away for a moment before turning back. "So I was planning to just sit here and do nothing and wait for my punishment."

"What was the punishment?" she asked.

"Oblivion," he said flatly.

Her heart sank, and her stomach twisted at the thought. "So you changed your mind?"

"I think so." He nodded. "I mean, it's scary to care again, but I really do. I care about you... and Bastien. And even some others." He twisted his fingers together. "I just... I'm bad at it still. When I left last night, I thought I was doing the best thing. I didn't know what it meant to leave." He gave her a hopeful look. "But if you'll let me, I'll stay tonight."

She felt hope welling up in her, filling her like a hot air balloon, making her feel floaty. "You want to?"

"Of course I want to," he said, folding his arms. "I wanted to last night. But as you've seen, I don't always have the best judgment, even when I'm trying to do the right thing."

"I know," she said. "I didn't react the best either."

They both smiled and then sat in awkward silence together. She took a deep breath. "Well, you were right. He was a creep."

"Yeah," he said. "But I could have been better about telling you about it."

She came over and sat next to him on the couch, and as he put his arm around her, she enjoyed the warm, soothing feeling that washed over her. That always did when he was around.

"What do you want to do tonight?" he asked. "I'm all yours, until you want to kick me out."

She laughed. "I wouldn't. Maybe just take it easy tonight? Watch a movie?"

He nodded. "Try that snuggling thing you were talking about." He wrapped both arms around her, encircling her with strong muscles. "I think that's what I missed most about leaving last night. I didn't get to hold you."

"I didn't know you wanted to."

"Of course I did," he said. "I always want to."

She smiled and gently pushed out of his arms.

"Well, in that case, you better help me make dinner so we can eat and get that out of the way. We've got some snuggling to do."

His blue eyes sparkled in a way she'd never seen before. Truly, it was like watching a black-and-white painting come into color the way he was changing every day.

"Sounds good to me."

CHAPTER 12

After dinner—where Luc had showed himself to be more than willing to help in the kitchen, if not woefully inexperienced with things as basic as boiling water—both of them returned to the living room to watch a movie as promised.

For the movie, Hallie chose something on the tame side, a romantic comedy with a little action sprinkled throughout. But as the movie began, Luc just sat next to her on the couch, sitting upright, his gaze darting from her to the movie, as if unsure of how to proceed.

Had Luc never done this before?

First, she nestled into him, leaning back on his

muscular frame, testing his reaction and seeing what he'd do next.

He maintained his upright position but looked down at her with a curious glance.

"You can relax, you know," she teased, poking him in the side, trying to get him to loosen up.

"I just want to make sure I'm doing it right," he said cautiously. It was kind of cute to think of this huge, overprotective guy taking *cuddling* too seriously.

"The key is to just find the right position for you and your partner so you can experience maximum comfort and enjoy the experience," she explained.

Luc made a *hm* sound, as if thinking for a moment. He then shifted his position, leaning into the back corner of the couch and then helping her move closer to him so she could rest back onto his chest, with the popcorn bowl in his lap before her.

Heaven.

"Ah, so *this* is cuddling," he said discerningly as he wrapped an arm around her side.

"Yes. And now we watch," she said, turning his attention back to the TV, more for her own sake than his. Every second those deep, multifaceted blue eyes watched her, every second his hands touched her anywhere, she could feel her skin warming, could feel her body's reaction to him.

As they watched, Hallie's mind wandered between paying attention to the TV, trying to ignore the rising sensations in her, and thinking about how radically different things were with Luc in her life. How even with the ups and downs, she didn't think there was anything she would change about it all.

"What are you thinking about?" Luc asked as he ran his fingers through her hair, his touch light despite the size of his hands.

"Just about how different things have been ever since you came. Now that things are so changed, I'm not sure I could go back to my life the way it was before."

"So you can see a future with me in it?" he asked thoughtfully.

"I mean, it hasn't been long, but if the present is any indicator of the future, then yes, I can only hope so," she said, turning back to see him looking down at her, his gaze tender and attentive.

"Me, too," he replied as she nestled back, moving the popcorn bowl to the floor so she could rest on his big, surprisingly comfortable lap.

"You're pretty good at this cuddling thing, by the way," she exclaimed, relishing the feel of his thighs beneath her and his arm resting on her side.

"Perhaps we should make it a regular thing, then?"

"Definitely."

As the movie finally wrapped up and the credits rolled, Hallie sat back up and stretched, yawning. Between their fight in the morning, the scene he made at her workplace, and the rescue right in front of her house, it had been a pretty long day.

"Here, let me get you upstairs," Luc said, sweeping Hallie off her feet and holding her in his arms, walking up the stairs toward her bedroom. "We can do some more cuddling in bed before we go to sleep," he said with a smile.

But as he took each step, there was definitely more than just cuddling on Hallie's mind. And it certainly didn't hurt that Luc had been the perfect gentleman the entire night, helping with dinner and holding her sweetly as if she meant the world to him.

Maybe she was just being stupid, lining herself up for more hurt. But she'd learned the hard way that no matter how careful you were in life, you could still get hurt regardless of what you did. So it was best to just live in the present and hope things turn out okay in the end.

"Um, Luc?" she said tentatively as he reached the top step and opened the door to her room.

"Yes?"

"If you're staying tonight, do you think we could do more than just cuddling?" she asked, feeling embarrassed by her delivery, but not sure how to bridge the subject smoothly.

"You mean go all the way this time?" he said bluntly, a smile quirking the corner of his lips.

She didn't reply, just nodded, her mind wild with thoughts of what that would entail.

Luc didn't reply immediately, but laid her on the bed, coming over her and straddling her with his powerful legs. He then leaned down, cupping the back of her neck with one hand and her cheek with the other as his lips touched hers in a powerful, soul-rocking kiss.

"How's that for my answer?" he asked, sitting up and looking down at her, his gaze now heated, the blueness of his eyes swirling like a fathomless whirlpool.

She could lose herself in those eyes, and she wouldn't even mind.

* * *

Luc thrummed with desire at this point. Both with the desire to be with her, and the powerful need to pleasure her, to own her and make her his.

Everything had gone perfectly. He hoped this was what their future would be like. Easy evenings full of fun conversation and new experiences. And nights bursting with heat and passion.

The kind of life Luc had never dreamed of being able to have, if not for Hallie.

He didn't waste time going slow tonight, though. He knew what Hallie wanted. And he wanted to give it to her. Wanted to give her everything, every part of himself he could offer. Everything they'd denied themselves the night before.

He pulled off Hallie's T-shirt and bra, followed by her soft sweatpants and underwear, leaving her bare to him so no clothes could stand between him and her pleasure. The sight of her naked was still astounding, still breathtaking.

This time, though, Hallie tugged restlessly at Luc's shirt, and he obliged by taking off his own clothes, satisfied with the way her eyes widened more with each article he removed, until there was nothing left to take off.

Immediately, he came back on the bed, his hands finding her soft breasts, his mouth covering hers in a ravenous, claiming kiss.

She moaned beneath him, her hands holding on to his thighs as he continued to kiss, touch, whatever he could do to fill her with as much pleasure as she could handle.

Already, he felt he'd known Hallie his whole life. Yet he could spend every night, every day, every second with her and still not have enough time; they were so perfect together.

He came lower and kissed her nipple, laving each of them with his tongue and then letting the cool air cause a firm tip to form before he kissed and sucked them again.

And maybe it had just been all the physical contact between them during the movie. Maybe it was just that they knew each other's bodies better now, knew each other better. But whatever it was, he could feel Hallie's first release quickly building, could tell she was already teetering near the edge.

He reached a finger between her legs and started to stroke slowly over her clit, continuing to use his mouth to full effect on her delicious breasts as she writhed beneath him, her long moans punctuating the air as she got closer.

Then with one last stroke, she came beneath him, her fingers digging into his legs as she called his name and tried her best to ride out the incredible experience of her orgasm.

Mate.

There was that voice again. His dragon saying

plainly what he clearly wanted.

Mate, mate, mate.

He tried to ignore the sound, but the sight of Hallie, the woman he was clearly meant to be with, stretching out on the sheets, her dark hair splayed all around her, beautiful and naked and always ready to receive more pleasure from him, was too strong to ignore.

For a moment, he twisted the sapphire ring on his finger, his heirloom, his gift for his one and only mate.

"I don't think I can handle all the lead-up," Hallie said with a happy sigh. "How about we skip to the main event?" she asked, her hands feeling along his chest, his abs.

"Whatever you want," he said, painfully aware of how hard he was for her, the reaction of his own body just as strong as hers was to his.

First, he slipped a finger inside her, then two, testing to make sure she could accommodate his sheer size. She moaned a little, but it was clear only one thing would fully satisfy her.

Once Luc was content she was ready, her slick

warmth erotic and inviting, he came close, ready to enter her. The air crackled with excitement as she watched him.

Then with one slow, long motion, he thrust into her.

The sensation was magical, tight and hot and everything he could have imagined. She gripped him from all angles, making the delineation between them seem nonexistent, making him feel he was wholly a part of her soul.

He slowly withdrew and then joined them again, enjoying the friction, and she gasped from the pleasure of it, the sensation.

Somehow, it was just perfect. Her soft, inviting warmth an unflawed contrast to the hard, unyielding side of him. Every time they moved together, it sent shocks of ecstasy through him, all the way to the tips of his toes and fingers.

It was so intimate. So wonderful.

There was no going back from this. He could never give her up.

And as he continued to thrust, Hallie wrapped her

legs around him, as desperate to keep him as he was to keep her.

Over and over, he came into her, holding for a second before moving out and then back in. And the more he did, the stronger and more vocal Hallie's responses became. Her hands wrapped into the sheets, pulled on her hair, looking for something to hold on to. So Luc held them for her, gripping her tightly as he continued to move, carrying them both toward the release their bodies begged for yet resisted at the same time.

And then Hallie began to move faster, thrusting her hips into his, and Luc found it very hard to maintain control. He started to go quicker, increasing his momentum as they came together over and over.

Luc could feel her getting nearer. Could feel the twitch of her muscles as she came so close he could almost taste it. With one final push, he went all the way into her, their bodies closer than ever before, as if one being.

And then she came, her hands gripping his as she arched back in ecstasy. A split second later, he was pulled into his own release, feeling his entire body awash in powerful pleasure that coursed through him in seemingly limitless amounts.

Even as their pleasure was replaced by sensual satisfaction, Luc didn't want to come out of her, didn't want the experience to end. If he could bottle it up and save it for eternity, he would.

But that's what life was all about, he guessed. Treasuring the good experiences and trying to make new memories, even better ones, with each new day.

Hallie relaxed back onto the bed and let out a long, contented sigh. The sight of her bare breasts and the glow of her pale skin and her happy, exhausted smile would be etched into his memory forever.

He leaned down to kiss her once more, then got up and cleaned off quickly in the bathroom, returning to the bed and covering them both with her sheets before curling around her.

"So *now* will you tell me what you really are?" she asked, yawning. It had been a long day. She'd had a lot to deal with.

"Not tonight," he said. "I just want to hold you."

"Okay," she said. "But soon?"

"Soon," he said. "Maybe tomorrow."

She murmured something and snuggled into him, muttering something about how he knew how to exhaust a woman. He curled around her tighter, as if with his body he could protect her from the whole world. Maybe he could.

"Hallie?" he asked quietly.

"Yes?"

"I love you," he said, surprised the words came so easily to him. But he knew what he felt. Knew what this was between them with certainty.

She turned toward him, more awake now, and gave him a sleepy smile. "I love you, too."

He brushed her hair back and gave her a kiss on the forehead. Pulling off his ring, he lifted one of her hands. "Will you be with me?" he asked.

"Like, officially?"

He nodded. "Yes. That's what I want. Wear my ring. Be mine." He knew he should be telling her more, but he could do that later. Right now, he knew this was right.

Her eyes sparkled as she looked at the ring, and then she put her hand out for him to slide it on. Everything in his heart was content as he watched it find a home at the base of her ring finger. Somehow, maybe through magic, it was a perfect fit.

She looked at it, turning her hand so it twinkled in the light. A shock went through him. She was his *mate*.

She lay back down and then reached up and pulled him over her, planting a kiss on his cheek. "And now I have to go to bed. It's been a long day. So snuggle me to sleep."

He laughed and lay down with her again, making sure the covers were perfect. She clapped, and the lights turned off. Very handy.

She fell asleep before he did, snoring lightly and muttering in her sleep.

"Sleep well, sweetheart. I'll make everything right in the morning," he said.

But as a shiver of nervousness moved through him, he wondered... Could he really?

CHAPTER 13

The next morning, Luc looked with wonder at his ring on his mate's hand.

He couldn't believe it had really happened. And so fast. But it had felt like the perfect timing, so why wait a moment longer?

The world was fickle and dangerous, so all the more reason not to wait when you met the one for you.

Not to mention, his ring could help her stay safe. He wasn't sure exactly what powers were contained there, but he knew it was the safest she could be.

Now there was just one thing left to do. Call the oracle and tell her to deactivate the collar. He was ready to be himself again and to align with humankind. Hallie had made him want to. Had brought back that kind part of himself, the part that thought it was possible to fight for what was right and succeed.

He tucked the covers around her and smiled at her soft snores as he left the room. He saw keys hanging up and took them so he could lock the door behind him.

When he was out on the sidewalk, the blinding morning sun beating down on him, he pulled out his phone and dialed the oracle's number.

"Hello? Luc?"

"Yes," he said, keeping his voice down so he didn't wake Hallie. Even though she was inside, he knew she was a light sleeper. He intended to tell her everything soon, but he had a specific way he wanted to go about it.

"What's going on? Is something wrong?"

"I found my mate," he said. "I want the collar off."

She was dead silent, and his heart pounded heavily as he waited. "Okay."

"That's it? You trust me? Do you even know—"

She cut him off. "I know you've been wanting to

be asleep ever since you made that terrible mistake. I know I've been waiting for you to forgive yourself and live again."

"I don't know about forgiving myself, but I'm ready to start making amends. I'm willing to start trying."

"I was never worried about restraining your power because I thought you would hurt humans," she said. "I restrained it because I thought you would harm yourself. Put yourself back to sleep."

He pressed his lips together. He had been fatalistic. Gloomy. Nothing to live for. Just wanting to return to oblivion. Amazing a mate could change all of that.

"How do you deactivate it?" he asked.

"Normally, I would have to touch it, but I can do it remotely. Give me a second."

He heard her set the phone down, rustling in the background, and then felt the necklace slip down his front. He caught it with one hand and stared down at it.

In a way, he was grateful for it. It had kept him safe until he could trust himself.

"So what are you going to do next?" she asked. "I'm glad to have you on our side. We can use your powers. All of them."

"You need rain?" he asked, laughing. "I mean, I don't think there are as many crops around here begging for it."

"Right, I forgot about your effect on weather. Maybe we won't need that as much, but we definitely will need your mass healing. Your freezing."

"Got it," he said. "Well, I'm at your disposal, like Zach, unless my mate is in danger."

"You gave her the ring, right?" she asked.

"Yes," he said. "Not sure what it'll do for her."

"You'll find out at some point," she said. "All that matters is you're with us. You're a very crucial dragon. I'm glad you came around."

"Thanks for waking me up and giving me a chance," he said. "It's been better than I could have hoped."

"Now just don't screw it up," she said with a laugh, and he hung up the phone.

He had somewhere to go. He looked down the

empty street and then got into his car to head over to the shelter. With the necklace off and the adrenaline of talking to the oracle over, he could feel power flooding through him again. A warm trickle that morphed into a deluge.

He was more keenly aware of his body, of the energy around him. And the water in the air.

Making it rain. With all the other powers he'd been thinking about, like healing and attacking, he'd totally forgotten how useful that used to be for humans. Sadness fell over him as he remembered how overjoyed those in his village had been whenever it fell for their crops.

Crops that had been burned to nothing.

But no, this wasn't going to be like that again. He wasn't going to let everything he loved be razed to the ground. He wasn't just watching humans, just checking in here and there. He was living among them, and he'd be there if shit went down.

When he arrived at the shelter, it was still early and everything was locked.

He took Hallie's keys that he'd used to lock her

door out of his pocket and let himself in, locking it behind him.

It was eerily quiet and dark, and he went through, flipping on lights.

He didn't know how to explain exactly to Hallie about himself, but he figured it couldn't hurt to start with one of his best qualities: his ability to heal.

And rather than explain it, he wanted to show her.

He walked over to Bastien's cage. He seemed to know something was different today, and he mewed slightly as Luc approached.

"Shh," Luc said. "I'm going to make everything better for you, buddy." He undid the cage and pulled Bastien out, loving the way the cat always snuggled in. He was really looking forward to being able to bring him home. The interesting little guy deserved a home like all the other cats, not to be cooped up in a cage.

Bastien stared up at Luc curiously, relaxing in his arms. Luc touched the lump on the cat's leg. He wasn't used to healing just one being or one area, but he was rusty, and it was a good place to start.

The only thing he couldn't do was raise the dead.

He touched Bastien's leg gently, and the cat jerked. He moved his hand over until he covered the lump completely, and then he closed his eyes and let soothing power wash through him. Felt warmth under his hand. Heard Bastien mew and then purr.

And then he felt clarity, as if a sort of darkness was gone, and he knew whatever was inside Bastien was no longer there.

Bastien hopped out of his hands and walked over the floor, shaking his leg behind him in a comical way. But there was no lump.

He mewed and jumped onto the bench, striding around like he owned the place, almost as if he were celebrating how good he felt.

He looked over at Luc and let out a long meow, like Bo did when he wanted attention. Luc grinned and sat down, and Bastien crept into his lap. "Want to come home with me now, buddy?"

The cat just pressed his face against him in answer, and Luc grinned. Then he looked at the rest of the pets in the cages along the wall. None were as sick as Bastien, but while he was here, he might as well help them, too.

Or maybe he was still nervous about going back and facing Hallie. What if she didn't accept him?

He walked over to the wall and held out a hand toward the animals, taking a deep breath. "Don't worry," he told Bastien. "This will just take a second."

* * *

Hallie couldn't believe how beautiful the ring was that Luc had given her. How things had changed in just one day.

He'd taken off again, but it was so different after he'd told her he loved her the night before and held her as they slept.

This time, she knew he'd be back and he wasn't just there for a moment. He was there to stay.

He'd said he'd hopefully explain everything today, and she was nervous but ready at the prospect. She got up, showered, and got ready all while keeping the ring on. It made her warm and happy, and she never wanted to take it off.

A part of her knew she should feel this was too good to be true. That it was some kind of obvious fantasy. But she also knew Luc was flesh and blood. She'd felt him inside her. He was as real as the air around her, and she couldn't wait to see him again.

She was just changing into some comfy clothes, a gray hoodie and black yoga pants, when the doorbell rang. Her back was a little achy, and she grabbed meds before heading down to the door. She was sure it was Luc.

Of course he'd be back soon. Maybe he was even bringing breakfast. Maybe they could eat while he updated her on everything.

She opened the door and gasped when she saw who was standing there, shadowed by the bright sunlight.

She couldn't make them out exactly, but none of them was Luc. None had his soothing presence. A prickle of trepidation moved up her back, and she tried to close the door again, but the man in front stopped it with his hand.

"Not so fast," he quipped, stepping forward into the house as she stumbled back. She turned to make a run for it, but he caught her around the waist. "Guys?"

he prompted, and the two men with him stepped forward, each catching her by the arm.

She looked desperately out the door to see if Luc was back by chance, but she didn't see him.

"Calm down," the lead man said, shutting the door behind him. "We have no interest in hurting you. We just need to know where the sapphire dragon is."

The men holding her shoved her onto her couch and sat on either side of her, making sure she didn't run.

Their leader sat gingerly in her usual chair, his posture arrogant, as if he were literally looking down on her, his legs crossed, hands resting on his knee. He had white-blond hair, shockingly light, and penetratingly green, almond-shaped eyes that tilted up at the sides. He could have been called handsome if there wasn't a distasteful cruelty to his features.

"Tsk-tsk," he said casually. "Unlike Sapphire, I rather like reading minds. And if you're going to say mean things about me, I might just do something mean as well."

"Who are you?" she asked, pulling free from the

men who still had ahold of her arms.

"Let her go," the blond man snapped, and his cronies obeyed. They were both tall and incredibly muscled, with dark-blond hair that reached their shoulders. But they looked nothing like the man across from her. He had an elegance, a thinly veiled power that sort of made you want to run.

He studied his nails. "Where is Sapphire?"

"I don't know what you mean," she said honestly.

His eyes dipped to her ring, and he grinned in amusement. "You mean he mated you and you don't even know what he is? Oh, that's rich."

She didn't know why he seemed amused, but she didn't like it. "What do you mean mated?"

He nodded at her hand. "The ring, darling."

"Don't call me that," she snapped. "And I don't know what you're talking about."

Blond dude cocked his head, a slight smile curving his lips meanly. "Isn't that tragic."

"Get out of my house," she said. "Whatever this *sapphire* is, he's not here. And what did you mean dragon?"

He looked at her sardonically. "What do you think I meant? I meant dragon. Fire-breathing, human-killing, powerful dragon. And I want him on my side."

"Are you talking about Luc?" she asked, agape.

He folded his arms and leaned back. "Is that what he's going by these days? I don't understand these modern names. Lucien was one name he used, I suppose. But given his powers, I think most just knew him as Sapphire."

She looked at her ring. "Like this?"

He nodded.

"So what are you? Emerald?" she asked.

His eyes glittered. "How did you know?" He stared at her, unnerving her. "But you can call me Aegis." His eyelashes were long. He really could almost be called beautiful if it weren't for his terrible personality.

"Tch. Almost a compliment, and then you had to go and insult me again," Emerald said. "Final warning. If you do it again, you'll see my powers. And unlike Sapphire, I'm not collared."

"That thing around his neck…?"

"Restrains his power, yes. Though, he probably has them back now. We have a mole in the oracle's place who said he was mated and would have his powers, so we came to see if we could get him on our side. Makes sense, right, given his nasty past?"

"I don't want you to tell me anything about him," she said, folding her arms. "He's coming back to talk to me, and we'll sort things out then."

"Right," Aegis said. "Because that's the proper order of things. Mating a woman and locking her to you forever and *then* telling her you're a ruthless monster. Makes sense."

"He's not a monster."

"Murderer, then," Aegis said.

She narrowed her eyes. She couldn't imagine Luc killing anyone. He was so *good*. But then just a bit of doubt crept it. She remembered how angry he got in fights. How violent.

"Luc wouldn't kill people," she said with certainty. She'd seen him use self-control. Sure, he might get scary mad, but someone always deserved it. And he hadn't gone too far. Much.

"You don't look like you believe that," Aegis said. "Anyway, what would be my reason for telling you? I wasn't here to have anything to do with you. I just thought he might want a chance to join our side simply because, with his past, he might be suited for it."

"Which side is that?" she asked skeptically.

"The opposite side of all the do-gooder dragons who want to help humans. Humans are hopeless. We're better off ruling them than trying to protect them."

"Luc doesn't think so," she said.

"I don't know," Aegis countered. "Maybe I know more about him than you. Still, I'm surprised he would mate you without telling you such an important part of his past."

"He can tell me what he wants, when he wants," she said. "Now you need to get out."

Aegis raised a blond eyebrow. "You don't get to command me, human."

"Luc isn't going to side with you."

"Maybe not. He's been living with Zach, the onyx dragon, my nemesis. A total weakling now that he's at the oracle's beck and call. Dragons were never meant to follow orders."

"Then who are you working for?" she asked. "Somehow I don't think you're doing this alone. You said you were on a side, too."

His bright-green eyes turned fiery, and he stood. "I do what I want, when I want. I work where I do because they're aligned with my interests, and if they're ever not, then I'll show them who is really in charge." He walked slowly toward her and knelt, bringing them eye to eye. Even his skin was gorgeous. He grinned.

"But let me tell you something, sweetheart. I may be one of the bad guys, but I've never mowed down a bunch of humans like Sapphire did." He cackled. "Not that I think he was wrong, but seriously. That was *cold*." He threw his head back and laughed at some inside joke as he stood.

He motioned for his guys to follow him as he walked to the door. "We'll be back when Luc is here," he said, opening it.

"He's here now," a deep voice said, and she heard a crack as Aegis was punched in the face and went stumbling back.

CHAPTER 14

When Aegis regained his feet, he was holding his face.

"Sapphire, what the fuck?" he asked.

Luc shook his hand as he stormed forward, shoving the cronies out of the way as he ran into the living room. His blue eyes were desperate, searching for Hallie.

"Luc!" she said, rushing over to him. After this unnerving encounter, she needed him. Just needed to feel his goodness, remind herself of who he really was.

He stepped back after a quick hug and handed her something that had been tucked under his arm.

It was Bastien, and he let out a meow as he came

over to her and tucked himself into a ball against her chest.

"What? You aren't supposed to…" She started babbling about the cat, but Luc put up a hand as he got between her and the guys standing by the door.

"Get out. If you come near my mate again, I'll kill you."

Aegis grinned his falsely charming grin again. "Right," he said, sharing a meaningful look with Hallie. "Because that's how you deal with things when you're angry. Right?"

Luc went still. "You're just trying to cause problems, and I want you out." He pointed at the door, but she could swear he was feeling something other than anger now. It seemed uncomfortably like… guilt.

Aegis couldn't have been telling the truth, could he? Given, it was a shock they were somehow dragons with incredible powers, and she needed to know more about that.

But Luc couldn't be a ruthless killer, could he? She couldn't imagine it.

"Ask him," Aegis said, staring. "Ask him if it's

true."

She didn't want to. She just wanted to cover her ears and keep everything the same. But the energy radiating from Luc wasn't right. And he was avoiding her eyes now, still facing away.

"Is it true?" she asked, still holding Bastien. She walked forward toward the man who had come to mean everything to her. "It isn't true, right?"

"What isn't true?" he asked in a flat tone.

"That you've killed people," she said. "Many people."

His shoulders dropped, and he still wouldn't face her. She grabbed him by his jacket with one hand and jerked him around.

As he faced her, she recognized a multitude of emotions on his face. Grief, disappointment, guilt. Nervousness. Anger when he glanced at Aegis.

"Oh, look at this. She's going to reject you," Aegis said. "Hilarious that you did all that, and now she's going to turn on you when she hears the truth." He folded his arms and nodded. "Well, when you feel betrayed and angry, you're welcome to come join us.

Heavens knows you're welcome."

"You did this on purpose," Luc growled.

Aegis put up his hands. "I did no such thing. I simply came to recruit you, since I figured, unlike Zach, you actually had claws. Given what I'd heard about you." He grinned, showing fang-like canines. "Anyway, I'll leave you to your mate." He reached in his pocket and pulled out a card, flicking it at them. It fluttered to the ground and neither of them reached for it. "Now you know where to find me."

Luc frowned, scowling at the other man as he took his leave, exiting with his cronies through the door.

Hallie and Luc moved to the window to watch them leave, and then she plunked down on the couch, drained.

He sat on the other end. "I was going to tell you," he said, rubbing his face with his hands. She set Bastien down so he could go find the other cats in the house, who all liked to hide in comfy places most of the time.

"Which would you have told me? That you were a powerful dragon, or that you mated me with your ring and it can't be taken back?"

"I told you I wanted you forever," he said.

"Or that you were a killer?" she choked out. "I didn't want to believe it. I wouldn't just from his lips. But looking at you when he said it, I knew. You did, didn't you?"

He nodded slowly, and she felt her heart crack in two.

"You didn't think I deserved to know that? To know who I was bonding myself to?"

"I did," he said. "I just didn't know how to tell you. There is so much."

She folded her arms. "Start at the beginning."

"I was born as a baby dragon—"

"Start with how you killed people!" she snapped, her heart racing.

He let out a long, frustrated breath, his body tense. "I didn't want it to be this way. I knew you would hate me."

"Then you should have told me and given me the chance," she said. "You've been in control of this thing all along. Leading me on. Chasing me and making me feel wanted. Asking me if I would love you if you were a monster. I thought that meant some mythical being. Not a killer!"

"I told you I was one of the bad guys."

"But you aren't!" she said. "I've never seen that in you. I know you're hard on yourself, but I never thought you were capable of something like that. It's not okay."

"Don't you think I know that?" he asked. "I've been torturing myself over it for many years. It's the reason I wanted to go back to oblivion."

"That won't bring them back," she said warily. "If you're this big, powerful creature, why did you need to kill humans? What could possibly make that right?"

She didn't know if she was angrier that he'd hidden all of this from her or that he'd mated her without telling her exactly what it meant. "It's one thing if you just happen to be something with powers. It's another to hide something that makes you a criminal."

He stood slowly, his hands on his legs. "So you want me to go?"

Her heart ached. Even through her anger, she

wasn't sure that was exactly what she wanted. But she was hurting, and it was hard to see through that.

It hurt her that Luc could hurt people.

It hurt her that he'd thought he didn't need to tell her what he was capable of.

"I just... can't believe you're the man I thought you were if you could hurt people like that."

"That was a lifetime ago," he said. "I'm not the man, or dragon, I was then."

"Then why did you do it?" she asked "What would justify it?"

He bit his lip. "It was stupid. I regret it every day."

"What was it? Why did you do it?" She had to know. She wanted badly for there to be a good reason.

But he stared at her. "I don't know what you want me to say."

"Say there was a reason. Say Aegis was lying! Say I haven't just been tricked into mating a murderer."

He just stared at her, and it made her angrier. Why wasn't he saying anything? Instead, he seemed lost in a haze. He folded his arms and turned away. "I thought you'd give me time to explain."

"I thought you'd know you should explain first, mate later."

"I thought you understood what the ring meant," he said.

"I didn't even know what you are! How could I understand anything?"

"Got it," he said dully. "So you want me out."

"For now," she said. "I need to think about this. I need to calm down." Pain shot through her. "I need to take more meds."

He took a step toward her, eyes going lighter. "Then before I go, let me show you one other part of me."

She was about to protest, but he closed the distance between them in a second, taking her in his arms. He spun her until her back was to the wall and took her lips in a deep kiss.

She tried to struggle, but he wasn't budging. But slowly, she realized this kiss was different than the others. His hands held her face, stroking gently, and she could feel energy flooding through her, as if he were breathing it into her body.

Her whole body felt lit up by warmth, and she felt tingling along her back, unlike anything she'd ever felt before. A warm, floating feeling that made her want to giggle. Her fingers dug into his back as her body went weak from the energy flowing through her.

When he pulled back, still holding her up, she could sense a ball of energy centered on her back, where her injury had been.

"You're probably right," he said quietly. "In that I could never deserve you. Never make right what I did. Never be anything but the killer I was." He helped her to the couch and then turned to swipe up the card Aegis had left on the ground. "But even if all of this just allowed me to help you and Bastien, it was worth it. Perhaps that's all it was."

"Wait," she said. "What do you mean help me and Bastien?"

"You'll get it soon," he said. "One of my powers."

"Where are you going? You aren't seriously thinking of joining up with Aegis?

He sighed and looked down at the card before tucking it in his pocket. "No, of course not." He gave her a sad look. "I've learned not to make decisions out of anger. I just took his card so we can keep track of him. Because I may have made a mistake, but he is working on the side of pure evil."

She didn't get a chance to answer before he headed out the door, shutting it behind him.

CHAPTER 15

Luc shut himself in his room as soon as he got back to the mansion, wanting to keep his icy rage as far from anyone else in the house as possible.

It had all been going fine before Aegis had shown up. He could have told Hallie about himself slowly. Could have made her smile to see Bastien better. Could have healed her and told her what he could do for mankind.

And then he could have gently told her his one big regret.

It was all coming back to him now. Remembering how out of control he'd felt that day. How all the love and hopelessness inside him had been unleashed on the band of robbers, laughing after murdering children.

He'd always been so peaceful, so controlled. Healing, bringing rain to dry areas, comforting others. Trying to get the other dragons to help.

He was known as the nice one, the kindest to people.

But in that kindness had been deep love that tore him asunder when it was violated.

He still didn't know what to do with those feelings. He would always feel guilty for those killings, even though they deserved it, and their deaths were quick and painless compared to the suffering they'd inflicted on a group of innocents.

It would have been one thing if they'd just engaged the men of the village in a fight, but they'd indiscriminately murdered women and children.

One human in particular had meant a lot to Luc. Anna. He tried to never think of her, but she came to him now. She'd been the first to approach him in his cave, not understanding who he was. Bringing bread to what she thought was a hermit.

He'd gotten to know her and came down to the

village to see it in a sorry state. Sickness. Starvation. He'd been able to solve a lot of it.

It had been his little experiment, and it was working. He was able to make a difference.

He'd been doing back then what the oracle was trying to get modern dragons to do now. He was helping.

And then one thing had gone wrong, and he'd turned into a monster.

He heard a quiet knock on the door and turned away. It felt like he was once again coated in ice, and he didn't want to share that with anyone.

The door opened, though, and Zach stood there, staring at him with dark, implacable eyes.

He walked in and sat on the edge of the bed, saying nothing at first.

Luc didn't know how to put it all into words, so he simply opened his mind and showed Zach his thoughts. What had happened with Aegis and Hallie. And then he shared his darkest memories so Zach could understand. The village burning. His icy breath bearing down with murderous fury.

Zach looked at him with sympathy in his dark eyes. "I'm sorry. I didn't know."

"You're sorry?" Luc asked. "For what? For me? I'm a killer. I don't deserve any apology."

"No," Zach said. "I'm sorry about your village. I'm sorry you lost all those people you cared about. Now that I care about someone, I can kind of understand how you must have felt."

Luc shook his head. "That doesn't excuse it."

"You know," Zach said. "I think it says something about your incredible love for humans, that even when you were painlessly ending a group of murdering pillagers, you felt it scar your soul."

"It doesn't make me happy to take any life," Luc said.

Zach folded his arms. "And that makes you kind of special. Because I can tell you if someone killed anyone I cared about, I'd annihilate them and wouldn't even feel bad about it."

"Well, you should. Two wrongs don't make a right," Luc said.

"We aren't perfect," Zach said. "We're dragons.

And if we're meant to be protectors, we aren't always going to get it right. Feelings get in the way. We aren't machines. You got angry. You did something impulsive for revenge. But guess what? Those men, do you think they would have stopped?"

Luc blinked. He hadn't quit beating himself up about it long enough to think about that.

"One thing you'll have to square with, once you forgive yourself, is being a dragon in this world doesn't always mean healing people and bringing rain. Sometimes it means fighting. Hurting. Even killing. Sometimes that's what is required to protect." He put a hand up. "And I know we shouldn't do it in anger. And I know the killing scarred your soul on a day when you were already wounded." He shook his head. "But it's not for us to decide who gets to be forgiven."

Luc nodded.

"One day, maybe there will be something that makes everything right. Balances things out and decides who is right and wrong and who needs to be punished." Zach raised his eyes to Luc meaningfully. "But that isn't now. Right now, the world needs you to forgive yourself and try to be better every day."

Luc nodded. "I've already changed. I've had chances to kill, and I've showed mercy. But what if something awful happened and I lost myself again?"

"You'll be with friends now," Zach said. "We won't allow you to lose yourself."

Luc let his eyes close, tears stinging his eyelids. So much pain. He supposed a part of himself had been berating himself over the killing so much so he didn't have to face the true injury.

Failing all those people who depended on him. Who he wanted to protect.

"If you'd gotten there sooner, you would have had to kill to protect them."

"They were laughing," he said, his voice hoarse through his tears. "They were laughing about murdering them." He put a hand up to his head. "Why do I have to feel so bad about killing someone when they could just laugh about it?"

Zach moved over next to him and sat beside him. "Because you are a good person, and that is a heavy burden for a good person to bear."

And then Luc let himself cry. Heavy, ugly tears. Turning inward to grieve the people he'd lost as their faces moved through his mind. He didn't want to let go of them. He didn't want them to be gone.

He hated that no amount of killing could bring them back.

"It's okay," Zach said, patting Luc's back awkwardly.

Luc choked out a laugh. "Is it? Is it okay? I'm a freaking mess. I've lost my mate. I'm only now dealing with my past. And Aegis is out there." He reached in his pocket and handed Zach the card. "He left this."

Zach took it, turning it over. "So he wants you to find him?"

"Yes," Luc said. "I think he thought if he could break things between me and Hallie, I would have no other option." He chucked the card aside. "As if."

"I think Hallie can still understand you," Zach said. "She might need time, but I bet Aegis made it sound worse than it was. And I bet you didn't correct it, because you're always beating yourself up."

"Hallie is an amazing person," Luc said. "She

forgave the people who took away so much of her life. She wouldn't understand the kind of rage I had."

"If she's is such an amazing person, she probably just needs time to get away from Aegis's mind control. You know how persuasive he is."

"He wasn't influencing her," Zach said.

"Still, he screwed things up. And as you showed me, he also made it seem like you intentionally trapped her, which you didn't. And from what you've told me in the past, Hallie really hates when other people make all the decisions."

"Yeah," Luc said, finally calming. "She does. So how do I fix it?"

"First, you make sure you understand yourself, so when you do go over there, you can explain in a truthful way. Not just a way that gets you beat up emotionally—like you think you deserve."

"Right," he said.

"Repeat after me," Zach instructed. "I'm a good person."

"I'm a good person," Luc echoed, rolling his eyes.

"My love made me angry, but I'm not ashamed of that love."

Tears bit Luc's eyes again. "I'm not ashamed of that love."

"Someday, maybe there will be a reckoning for my actions."

"Someday, there may be a reckoning for my actions.

"But for now, I'm going to forgive myself for what I did when I was hurt and move on with my life."

As Luc repeated that last line, he felt lightness inside him. He let out a sigh and stood and stretched.

He looked over at Zach. "Thank you. I'm feeling better. I think."

"No problem," Zach said. "I owe you. My whole life, you were always preaching about humans and how they were worth our time. I think maybe that helped me when I met Erin. For that, I'll owe you forever."

Luc swallowed. "And I you."

"Well, you can pay me back by never joining with Aegis," Zach said.

Luc scoffed. "Already done."

"Good," Zach said. "Now let's get you cleaned up and send you over to get your mate back."

* * *

It was minutes after Luc had left before Hallie finally let the tears come.

She wasn't sure what exactly was bothering her so much. Maybe it was that she had always wondered if it was too good to be true that he'd come into her life. Maybe him being some kind of murderer was the only thing that made it better.

She blinked as she realized the warm ball inside her was finally starting to subside.

Such an odd sensation. And it had been so weird for him to force a kiss on her like that. Normally, he would have let her go. But he was insistent, almost desperate.

She sighed. One side of Luc was thoughtful, caring, almost too sweet. But there was also the other, angrier side she had seen. Scary, intimidating. Out of control.

Or was he?

He'd never lost it around her, only protecting her.

Perhaps she should have waited to see if he could explain better, but when he hadn't been willing to defend himself at all, it had made her angry.

Because surely, if he cared about her, he would give her any good motive he had.

So it stood to reason that he didn't have one.

Either that or he didn't *think* he did. She bit her lip as she acknowledged his tendency to beat himself up. She really should have given him a chance to explain.

But she hated hearing all about him from someone else. And she hated feeling like he'd taken her choice away. That almost made it seem like he'd done it on purpose. Like he'd thought she wouldn't accept him if she knew everything, so he'd tried to take that away the possibility.

But that didn't sound like the Luc she knew.

It was more likely that he'd gotten caught up in the moment and then been putting off telling her anything because he was afraid. He kept everything inside, to his own detriment; that much she knew about him.

She saw Bastien creep out from behind the couch with a soft mew, and she patted her leg for him to come over.

She didn't know what Luc was thinking, going to the shelter so early, getting a sick cat out. She grabbed Bastien when he came close, lifting him onto her lap, and gasped when she looked down at his leg.

The bump was gone. It was unmistakable.

She ran her finger over where it had been. There was no sign of it. Was she just imagining things?

No, she'd known Bastien was sick. Had grieved over it. She'd seen the X-rays, the ultrasounds.

Bastien looked up at her curiously, as he if he wasn't sure what she was getting so worked up about.

She remembered Luc had been holding him. Always concerned with him. She thought about the warmth in her back.

She stood, setting Bastien down, and prepared to do a move she hadn't been able to complete in ten years. Ever since her injury, she'd been able to minimize her pain by delineating specific movements that were and weren't okay. She was going to do one of the not-okay ones now.

She bent quickly down and then snapped back up, flattening her back.

No pain.

Tears came immediately, and she sat on the couch, gasping and covering her mouth in shock. She looked over at Bastien, now happily hopping up onto a chair and grooming himself.

This was what Luc had meant by his powers. She hadn't even given him a chance to show her that side of himself. She'd just chased him off, hurt by his secrets.

Aegis had said something about the collar being gone and Luc having his powers back. It said something about him that the first thing he would do with all of that power was go to heal a sick little cat.

He'd probably hoped he could come bring her Bastien and explain everything.

And she'd let that evil prick come in and ruin things, when they were so close to their happy ending.

Perhaps there were complicated aspects to Luc. But just as there might be a really dark side to his past, she also knew there had to be a light one. Because his first instinct when getting power back was to heal, not hurt. That was the Luc she knew.

She stood and paced, unsure what to do. Should she go talk to him? Apologize for jumping down his throat? Tell him it had all been overwhelming for her, too? And that she was scared, after all these years alone, that she'd be taken advantage of? That everything that felt so amazing would turn out to be too good to be true?

No, she didn't know what to say. Or if he'd even want to see her. Or where he was living. He'd always come to get her, not the other way around.

She sat back down with a huff. Then she heard another knock at the door. She got up hesitantly to look through the peephole, and when she saw the blond douchebag from before, she rolled her eyes and did the deadbolt.

"Undo it," a sharp voice called out.

She gasped as she felt her body move against her will, unlocking the deadbolt, no matter how much she tried to resist.

"Ah, so now you're seeing one of my powers,"

the voice said. "Now unlock the other lock and open the door."

She did as he asked, her heart hammering against her chest like a woodpecker.

"Invite me in," he said smoothly, his green eyes glowing like a snake's.

"Come in," she said shakily.

He did so, looking around.

"Where are your goons?" she asked.

He rubbed his hands together. "I only needed them if I was dealing with Sapphire. With you, I can just ask."

She frowned. "What do you want?"

He shrugged. "I just need Sapphire to come with me. Unfortunately, I saw he took off for Zach's place, and I just can't have that. Not when he could be so good with us." He eyed her. "So I've come to the conclusion there is only one way to get Luc to come to us. And that's taking you."

She tried to let out a squeak of shock as he reached for her, but he held up a finger.

"Shut up. Follow me," he said, leading her out of

the house. She followed, feeling like invisible strings were threaded through her, controlling her motions.

He opened the door to his car. "Get in."

She did, looking at him with fear.

"Oh, for Pete's sake, I won't hurt you." He went around and got in on his side, doing up his seatbelt. "Now text him. Beg him for help. Make it sound bad." He grinned. "Let him know I have you."

She pulled out her phone, gritting her teeth in frustration as her fingers moved on their own, flying over the keyboard, tapping out a message that would surely terrify Luc.

"Good," he said. "Now, we've got a long drive, so I want you to just be quiet. And no freaking out."

She would have scoffed at that if she could have. Ugh. Who did this guy think he was?

"The emerald dragon," he said, answering her silent thoughts. "The biggest, baddest dragon of all." He winked at her. "At least for now."

She rolled her eyes and leaned against the window, hoping whatever happened when Luc got the message, he would be careful and safe.

SAPPHIRE DRAGON

CHAPTER 16

Luc and Zach were eating, trying to get Erin's opinion on what he should do as far as winning Hallie back, when his phone beeped.

He absentmindedly brought out the phone, wondering who would be texting him, since he never used his phone, and he saw a message from Hallie that made his blood ice over almost instantly.

"Need help. Taken by Emerald."

He slammed the phone down on the counter and started for the door, pulling on a jacket.

Zach ran after him, trying to stop him by jerking on his arm. Luc glared at him, rage in his eyes.

"Emerald has Hallie," he said, angry with himself

as much as he was with Emerald. He shook his head. "I really thought he was only after me. Waiting for me to come to him. With his powers, I don't want to think about what he could do."

"Hold on," Zach said. "He's a jerk right now, yes, but he's not going to hurt your mate. He has never had any beef with you, unlike with me."

Luc sighed. "I'm not betting on anything when it comes to Hallie. I need her back. I need to make things right."

"You won't be able to make things right if you walk into a straight-up trap," Zach reminded him. "You have no idea who Emerald is working for or with. There could be many, many people helping him."

"I don't care. He has my mate," Luc said.

"All right, but I'm going with you," Zach said.

They both looked at Erin, who was staring worriedly at them from the kitchen.

"Be safe," she said.

Zach strode over to her, dipped her in his arms, and kissed her. "Of course I will. I'm invincible, remember?"

"I know," she said. "But you're everything to me."

Luc couldn't even roll his eyes at what they were doing, because he wanted that with Hallie. And he was going to have it as soon as he got her back.

He'd freeze them all where they stood and reclaim his mate.

Zach grabbed a few things, and they headed out to get in his truck. They set the GPS to the address on the card, and it came up with a travel time of a few hours.

"That's not going to work," Luc said in exasperation, getting out of the truck and slamming the door.

"Hey," Zach said. "Come on. I promise he's not going to let them hurt her. I know him. He hates me more than anyone. He doesn't just hurt random people."

"That was before he woke up. Before he started working with whatever evil piece of shit he's working for."

"I know, I know," Zach said. "But come on. I have the route down well enough after looking at the

GPS. We can just fly. It'll be much faster being able to go direct and bypass all the winding mountain roads."

"Great," Luc said, striding out onto the main lawn with Zach. It was good he had such a large, private house with expansive grounds. Luc would buy the same thing after he visited his treasure trove.

"Still remember how to shift?" Zach asked, slowly morphing in a dark-black cloud, taller and taller.

"Of course," Luc said. "It's what I am. The human is the disguise." He closed his eyes and listened internally, felt rushing energy and then his body growing, expanding past its cramped confines.

When he opened his eyes, he was so tall, and the air around him was crystalline, icy. He spread his giant blue wings with a grin. Then he flapped them, rising into the air alongside Zach's giant, sparkly black dragon.

When they were high enough, they took off into the clouds where no one could see them, flying at top speed.

If it hadn't been for his panic, it would have been amazing to fly again, watching mountains and trees pass by in a blur below him. Watching the clouds change color and thickness, feeling the cold air on his scaly body.

He wished he could have showed Hallie his dragon on his first transformation. Maybe he'd still get to.

He had no idea where they were going, so he followed Zach, trying to keep his mind off what could be happening to her while they travelled.

After a couple hours of straight flying at top speed, he was beginning to tire, just as Zach started to slowly descend toward some mountains in the distance.

They flew lower until he could make out little mountain roads and a small sort of compound in the distance, nestled in a valley at the center of the peaks.

Unless you came at it from an aerial view or happened to drive the winding, obscure roads leading to the compound, you'd never know it was there.

Given the fact that Zach was aiming straight at it, that had to be where they were keeping Hallie.

They flew in a circle until they saw a safe place to land outside the compound, and then they hit the ground hard, their claws raking the dirt as they slowed themselves after their long flight.

"Holy shit," Zach said. "I'm already tired."

"Are you, though?" Luc said, shifting back to his human and cracking his knuckles. Aside from flight, he could use all his dragon powers in this form. And his human form was less tiring to maintain.

"No. Not now that we get to fight," Zach said, shifting back as well. One of the benefits of being a dragon shifter was the ability to stay clothed between shifts due to the higher level of magic. Thus, Zach was still wearing his usual leather jacket and dark jeans.

And Luc was wearing the tee shirt and jeans he'd left home in, under a gray jacket.

They looked up at the first wall into the compound.

"Well, they wanted us here. Now they have us," Zach said.

"We didn't want both of you," a sardonic voice said over the loudspeakers. "Just Sapphire, you dick."

"I think he means me," Zach said. "Same to you, asshole!" He raised a bird in the direction of the speaker, and Luc raised an eyebrow.

"I'm pretty sure that means something sexual *and* offensive," Zach said, grinning.

Luc took a step forward. "Where is Hallie?"

"You just need to come up and talk to me," Aegis said through the speaker. "Just hear me out, and I'll give your mate back. Safe and sound." There was rustling. "You're safe and sound, right, darling? Tell him you're safe and sound," Aegis said, clearly talking to someone else.

"I'm safe and sound," said Hallie's voice through the speaker, sending both rage and relief through Luc. Relief because she was fine. Rage because Aegis was controlling her.

"I won't talk until I see Hallie," Luc called out.

"Well," Aegis said as a whirring, creaking sound started. "I guess we can talk about that in a minute. But first, I have someone here who wants to see you still have your powers."

"What the fuck…?" Luke trailed off as the cement doors in front of them were slowly pulled apart, revealing a courtyard.

Inside the yard were dozens of tall, strong-looking men, all wearing black, some of them carrying modern-looking weapons.

Whatever they were doing up here in the mountains, whoever Emerald was working for, they were raising an army by the looks of it.

An army of shifters, according to the various scents in the air. But they didn't smell right, and he couldn't make out exactly what type. Like something was off about them.

But he didn't have time to figure it out. He just needed them out of his way.

A bolt of lightning struck nearby, followed by the clap of thunder and the applause of heavy rain as it clattered to the earth all around them.

"I never was too fond of your ability to do that," Zach said sarcastically, looking up at the suddenly darkened sky and back to his quickly soaking leather jacket.

"Let's just take care of these guys and find Hallie," Luc snapped, ignoring Zach's comment and seething with indignant fury.

One particularly tall man stepped forward, at least part bear from the looks of it, and judging by his posture, probably a leader of some sort.

"Move out!" he shouted, and the men around him began moving forward in ranked groups, approaching cautiously, weapons raised.

Aegis's voice came over the loudspeaker. "Capture the ice dragon. Do whatever you like with the other. Something painful preferably."

"Be careful. Not everything they have looks manmade." Zach cracked his knuckles and stepped forward.

"I don't think we'll need to worry about it," Luc said, taking in a deep breath and feeling ice flow through his veins, his body changing shape once again into his dragon, adrenaline and rage mixing with cold, calculated resolution to save his mate.

If he didn't have to, he'd prefer to not kill anyone. But all bets were off now. He'd squared with what happened in the past, and all he had now was the firm resolve to protect his mate, no matter the cost.

Immediately, the men approaching began firing,

and Luc focused the rain in front of him, concentrating it and creating a solid wall of ice.

Go time.

He charged through the ice wall, right into the center of the unsuspecting soldiers. As the wall crashed all around them, sending the men scattering in different directions to avoid the debris, Luc breathed his dragon fire all around, a thick white stream of ice that froze anything too slow to avoid it.

With the path clear, he charged into the compound, swatting one soldier and then another with his gigantic talons, throwing them headlong into nearby buildings and walls.

"I forgot how fun it is to watch you in action," Zach said, following in right behind him and swiping a monstrous black claw at a nearby tower, knocking it over and sending the men on it careening into the nearby tree line.

By now, the entire compound was awash in commotion and gunfire. More men poured into the center through doors that ran deeper into the buildings adjoining the main perimeter.

Along the walls, men filed onto catwalks in an attempt to surround them from all sides, while others ducked into Humvees and began driving, circling the two huge dragons occupying the main courtyard.

CHAPTER 17

Whoever was behind this meant business.

But so did Lucien.

He breathed his dragon fire once again, this time on the heavy rain droplets around him, freezing them and sending them flying at high speeds like ice daggers all around him, focusing on the men along the walls in particular. Those who didn't duck or jump for cover were given something to remember him by.

Thankfully, these men seemed equipped with armor and other protective gear, so unless he made a point of killing them, they'd survive. Probably.

The men in the vehicles below them drove wide circles, moving fast and trying to stay clear of Luc's and Zach's spiked, dangerous tails as they swung at them. Then without warning, Luc felt explosions going off around him, some flying wide and missing, but others detonating dangerously close as men fired from weapons mounted on the tops of the Humvees.

And unlike Zach, Lucien didn't have invulnerable onyx skin, though his enhanced healing made it so he was pretty damn hard to hurt for long, let alone kill.

He stamped down and crushed a car that came too close to his claws. Then all of a sudden, to Luc's right, a huge green figure slammed into the onyx dragon, pushing him into a wall that cracked and groaned under the force of it.

"You didn't think I'd miss out on all the fun, did you?" the emerald dragon sneered, his beast not quite as big as Zach's, but still formidable.

"So you were thinking about me?" Zach grunted, a low rumbling sound, as he pushed the huge green dragon off and swiped his black, stone-rimmed tail at him.

"Thinking of ways to end you, yes," Aegis replied viciously, dodging backward and then squaring off with him, bright-yellow eyes focused on his age-old nemesis.

But Zach could handle Aegis.

Luc needed to clear a path so he could go looking for Hallie. The only thing that mattered was knowing she was okay, knowing she was safe. And the only way he could be certain of that was if she was in his arms.

He focused his energy on the sky above them, and a second later, huge boulders of ice came falling down, crashing into the last few parked vehicles and ripping through walls and windows.

Where there was water, there was hail. And where there was hail, Luc could make bigger hail.

Most of the men still in the courtyard ducked for cover beneath the onslaught of raining destruction. And as they scattered, Luc moved through them, tossing them like rag dolls or freezing them in place and immobilizing them.

To the left, a large door opened, and a tightly packed group of men marched toward him, wielding tall, gray shields and long, forked poles that clacked and popped with electricity. Lucien breathed a long cone of ice on them, but somehow, the shields remained unfrozen, unaffected.

That was definitely a first.

Whoever created this technology made it with dragons in mind.

Ignoring the swipes of their electric spears, Luc charged headlong into the group, letting his long horns and the spikes along his skull do the talking instead.

The men shrieked and dodged, to no avail, as most were caught by the assault and thrown back through the door, piling into each other or hitting walls with incredible impact.

Despite all of the collisions, Luc didn't think he had killed anyone, based on the energies around him, and that was an exhilarating feeling. Having power *and* control.

With the newest group cleared, by now most of the fighting was starting to quiet, and only the sound of the rain and a few hysterical, fleeing men could be heard, punctuated by loud thuds and crashes as Onyx and Emerald duked out their ancient grudge match.

But just as Aegis and Zach were clinched,

wrestling and swinging their gigantic tails, Aegis leapt back with a muttered curse, looking skyward.

"I'm being called back," he said, looking supremely disappointed." He shot up into the air and hovered for a second, glaring down at Zach. "I'll have to kick your ass later."

With that, he pushed off the ground and flapped his wings, rising into the sky and disappearing into the thick storm clouds close above them.

"Come back here, you bastard! We were just getting started!" Zach said with a roar, breathing his dark, diamond-like breath into the sky in vain, the rainclouds too near and too thick to see through.

"Sorry to disappoint. Another time, another place," he said, his voice calling faintly across the distance.

Zach huffed and then turned back to Luc. "I'll take care of the stragglers. You go get your mate," he said, swiping away a roaring, snarling shifter that was viciously biting and scratching at his leg.

Apparently, that guy hadn't gotten the message that the fight was more or less over.

Luc shifted back into his human form as he began running toward the biggest doors he could see, ones that led into what looked like the side of one of the mountains surrounding the compound. Behind him, he could hear Zach let out a roar of triumph as he cleaned up.

Whatever Emerald's crew was planning, they would know they needed more than that to take on dragons.

He ran down a long, metal-lined corridor, trying to pick up on the scent of his mate or hear her thoughts.

Luc. Luc, are you out there? Are you okay? Stay safe.

Her thoughts touched him. Even after what she'd been through, even after their fight, she was worried for him. And thankfully, she was apparently doing well enough that she could.

Zach had been right. Emerald wouldn't hurt his mate. Perhaps there was something redeemable about him.

Luc made a left turn, astonished at the sheer size of the place despite its relatively low profile from the outside, and came upon a pair of guards in front of a large, steel door.

As he approached, the bored-looking soldiers eyed him suspiciously. Then one man's face contorted in surprise and recognition as he walked up to them.

"Hey, that's the guy we're supposed to—"

The man's exclamation was cut off, though, as Luc swung a powerful punch into his jaw, sending him flying into a stack of metal crates that clattered with incredible noise. The other man immediately charged, but Luc just picked him up and tossed him into the neighboring wall, where he ricocheted off and landed on the ground with a grunt.

"Luc, is that you?" Hallie called from the other side of the door, muffled through the thick metal.

He pressed a red button that looked like it might operate the door, but a small screen simply displayed the words "access denied" in red type. He tried again and got the same response.

Screw that.

"Yes, it's me. Just get clear of the door, okay?" he said, followed by the sound of footsteps moving away from the door on the other side.

With a grunt, he pulled at the doors, wrenching them open despite their size and weight. When they yielded an inch, then two, he could see inside a small room full of panels with bright-colored buttons and TV screens and, in the center, his mate, Hallie.

Seeing her invigorated him even more, and he pushed against the doors, one hand on each, grateful for his dragon strength, since the corridors would be far too small to fit his full-sized dragon form.

Once the doors finally ripped opened, the supports holding them giving way and shattering, he stepped inside, and Hallie rushed forward to meet him. He caught her in his arms and held her tightly.

"Are you all right? Did they do anything?" he said, worried to death something might have happened in the time it took him and Zach to fly here.

"No. I'm okay. You got here soon after us," she replied, the sound of her voice more soothing than anything else in the world.

"Are you certain?" he asked, still paranoid, still over the moon to have her once again with him.

"I mean, aside from Emerald, or Aegis, doing that scary mind control thing to bring me here, nothing else happened."

Luc put *stomp Aegis silly* on his list of things to do when he saw him next. No one got away with doing *anything* to his mate.

"Honestly, though, I'm fine. Are you? It sounded like the apocalypse out there," she said, her arms wrapped around his midsection, the height difference between him and his curvy mate all the more apparent.

"Now that I have you, everything is better," he said, picking her up in his arms and walking back in the direction from which he'd entered the compound earlier.

Hallie just rested her head on his shoulder as he quickly trotted back along the path and into the courtyard. When they arrived, the scene of chaos was even worse than Luc remembered, and Hallie gave out a gasp of surprise.

"Did you do this?"

"With my friend's help, yes," he said, nodding to the huge black dragon looming over a pack of cowering soldiers with their hands above their heads.

Everywhere there were boulders of ice or piles of rubble or patches of frozen ground where his breath had touched. Then as they came up to Zach, the onyx dragon looked over and smiled, though the rows of dark, razor-sharp teeth did nothing to improve his terrifying appearance.

"So this is what dragons look like?" Hallie squeaked in shock. Is this what you *look* like?" she asked, turning to Luc.

"Not exactly. You'll see in a moment," he said, putting her down for a second. "What are you planning on doing with these guys?" he asked Zach.

"I gave the oracle a call. The blue and red dragon pair were actually in the area, so they'll be here any minute to join me. So you just get your mate home and let us take care of it."

"You did all this… for me?" She looked mildly horrified.

"We didn't kill anyone," Zach said. "Then again, they were all shifters, so it's easier. But Luc here did good keeping himself in check. He was precise while still being a total monster."

She hooked an arm through his. "My monster."

He gazed down at her, unsure if he'd ever heard anything more wonderful than being called hers.

"Are you ready to fly?" he asked, turning to her.

"Fly?" she said, confused.

Luc backed away from her until he was at a safe distance and then shifted one last time into his dragon, towering and immortal. Below, he saw Hallie's eyes go wide in amazement, then delight as she walked up to his leg and ran her hand along the scales there.

"Wow. So this was really you the whole time? Kind of hard to believe," she exclaimed.

"Yes. I'm sorry I didn't know how to tell you sooner. I—"

"It's okay." She interrupted before he could keep babbling. "Let's go home."

"Yes. Home," he said, picking her up gingerly to put her on his neck. "You okay?" he asked. "Hold on to my scales. I'll make sure you don't fall."

"Okay," she said, sounding nervous but holding on tight.

He let out a roar and then pushed off the ground and headed into the sky, dispersing the once-black rainclouds before them and heading into the clear, blue horizon.

Home couldn't come fast enough.

CHAPTER 18

He flew them back to Zach's place because there was more cloud cover and then a large amount of land to come down on. Dragons could be invisible as needed, but sometimes, if someone looked in the right spot, they could see something shimmering in the air, so they had to be careful.

He was still reeling from the amount of power he'd wielded today. Unlike the past, where his attack had felt out of control, toxic, terrible, today he'd felt strong, powerful. In the right.

He supposed both sides of him had a purpose, as long as they were used correctly.

There was the healing side, warm and loving and

helpful. But if anyone messed with his mate or his people or shifters, there was the other side that could rain (literally) righteous justice on the bad guys.

Hopefully, he would keep learning to understand both.

Hallie at least seemed to accept both sides of him. Though they'd fought, she hadn't said anything about it since he'd showed up to rescue her.

As they landed, Erin came running out on the lawn, reddish-brown hair flowing out behind her. "Where's Zach?"

"He's fine," Luc said, giving Erin a quick hug of comfort. "He'll be back soon. Just taking care of clean-up."

"Zach?" Hallie asked.

"The black dragon you saw," Luc replied.

Hallie looked from Erin to Luc, and it clicked. "Zach from the shelter? He's a dragon, too?"

Erin walked forward and folded Hallie in her arms. "Welcome to the dragon family."

Hallie blinked, and then her gray eyes went warm and she wrapped her arms around Erin. "Thanks for having me."

Erin led the way back inside, eyeing Luc, who looked a little worse for wear after all the fighting. There were black smudges all over his skin and little tears in his clothing. "You two go ahead and clean up," Erin said. "I'll go make something to eat." She grinned at Hallie. "And congrats on mating."

Hallie's expression shuttered slightly but she nodded. "Thank you."

Luc took his mate by the hand and led her up to his bedroom, not stopping until they were in and he could close the door. He sat on the bed with a huff and pulled her in to stand between his legs. "Finally."

She looked down at him, her long lashes sultry over her gray eyes. "So are we going to talk, or should I just thank you for saving me and call it a day?"

"We should talk," he said. "I didn't explain things well."

She kept his hand in hers and sat next to him on the bed. Outside the window, rain began falling. "That's odd."

He grinned. "Something I just like to do. It'll

probably be raining a lot since I haven't been able to use it in a long time."

She stared. "You can make it rain? What else can you do?"

"Mostly that and healing," he said, leaning back. "And then I have tactical stuff I can do with my ice."

"Ah," she said. "I guess I'll figure it out as we go. It's all fine with me."

"Hallie, about me killing people. I need to talk to you about it."

"Sure," she said. "But I already figured out I shouldn't have let Emerald get in my head. I should have known you needed more time to defend yourself, given your propensity to beat yourself up."

"It happened before I went to sleep," he said, trying to hurry and get it out before he lost his nerve. "A village was destroyed. Not just any village, one full of people I loved. I don't think I even let myself acknowledge how much I loved them. I told myself it was just an experiment. To see if dragons could intervene with humans in good ways. Ways that made a difference."

She listened quietly, attentively. It only made him love her even more.

"One day, I was flying back to see if their crops had enough water, to see if anyone was sick, and everything was ruined. Burned to the ground. Everyone dead."

Her jaw dropped. "What?"

"Murdered," he said. "Kids. Women. Innocent people." He ran his fingers through his hair as she placed a hand on his leg, soothing him. "I went into a rage. I guess that's when I woke the icy side of me. I found the attackers. I killed them. I didn't even hesitate. There was too much rage. It was so fast. When it was over, I couldn't take it."

"But they were murderers," she said, rubbing his thigh.

"I know. But I don't like killing. Zach has helped me understand it may happen, even in this new world where things are supposed to be safer. And I get that now. If I want to intervene, I have to use my strength in multiple ways. But I will always prefer to be a healer."

"I'm sorry you went through that," she said

quietly, reaching over to take his hand. "And I'm sorry I judged you. I guess ever since you came into my life, it has felt too good to be true. If you were some kind of monster, I guess it would have made more sense why you were with me."

He tilted her chin up so he could look at her. "Stop it. You're too good for me. You're the reason I wanted to be better." He released her with a sigh, looking back at the window where the rain was abating. "Before that, I just wanted to die. After I killed those people, I was restless. Angry. I fought other humans. Other dragons. I just sort of lost that other part of me. And then I was captured, put on ice. I didn't even mind when I knew it was going to happen. And when I woke up, I was angry. What was the point?"

He put his arm around her. "But then I met you, struggling with your pain, putting it aside to help others, and you made me want to wake that other side of me again. You made me want to heal and care and love again. You made it easy to love you."

"I can't believe you healed me. And Bastien. He looks great."

"Yeah," he said. "Wherever we live, I hope we can bring him."

"Well, I did say if he ever got better, he was yours," she said.

"And are you okay with that?"

"He's probably still getting acquainted with my kitties, but I'm sure they'll work it out," she said. "There are a lot of things to work out, but it's worth it."

"So you forgive me?" he asked. "For mating you, for keeping secrets?"

"Of course," she said. "And you forgive me for going off?"

"Nothing to forgive," he said, looking at the ring on her finger. "I was selfish for pushing you into that without fully explaining. I was just caught up in the emotion of it."

"I understand," she said.

They just sat there for a moment, resting, enjoying the warmth, and listening to the barely pattering rain outside the window.

Then, without asking, he leaned her back onto the bed and went with her, kissing her passionately.

She stroked his hair, and he wrapped his fist around some of hers, keeping her close. She moaned as he tilted her head back and kissed her neck, licking his way to her collarbone, grazing the sensitive skin just above her breasts.

"You're mine," he said, grabbing her hands and pinning them above her head. "Say it."

"I'm yours," she said plainly. "I have been from the moment I met you."

He grinned, flashing a fang, and lowered himself over her.

* * *

It was different this time, making love to him.

Each time Hallie felt his touch, it was unique. She hoped there would be a million days like this, experiencing new ways of loving each other's bodies.

Today he was slow and languorous, taking time to explore with his tongue as his hands traveled her body. He'd let her hands go the moment she'd said she was his.

It felt so right saying it. It was easy giving in to him.

Even after seeing the results of his power in the destroyed compound where she'd been held, she'd felt only awe for him.

And now that she knew more about what he'd been through, she loved him even more.

"You're everything," he said. "You're my entire world."

She laughed and arched as he placed more kisses up her neck and behind her ear, making her shiver deliciously. "I don't even know what to say to that."

"Say you're mine. I can't hear it enough. Say you'll never let anyone else do this but me."

"I'm yours," she murmured in his ear, enjoying the way his body tensed as her breath brushed his skin. "No one but you gets to do this with me."

He sighed in satisfaction and went back to kissing her neck, his hands slowly removing her shirt as he did so. First peeling off the hoodie as she helped get her hands out of it, then sliding off the tank top. She sat up and unhooked her bra, throwing it on the carpet, as he pulled his shirt over his head, revealing magnificent abs.

"So hot." She sighed.

He simply wrapped them together, chest to warm chest, and ran his hands over her shoulders and arms as he kissed her again, just under the ear, and then took her earlobe between his lips, gently biting down.

She arched and gasped, and he quickly pulled off her pants and then raised a hand. He flicked out a blue claw, and she saw the light glint off of it just for a second before he hooked it around her panties and tore them right off.

"I've been wanting to do that," he said. "But I couldn't until you knew what I was."

"Pervert," she muttered.

"Yes," he said, closing his lips around a nipple. "But only for you."

"Perfect," she said, letting out a moan as he moved to her other breast, licking and then biting gently.

His hands were on her thighs now, kneading the skin there as she felt tension building inside her. She was here and spreading her legs for him. There was no one else she wanted this way, but she wanted him badly.

He looked down, heat in his blue eyes, smudges on his cheeks, blond hair damp and mussed, and stood up off the bed to remove the rest of his clothes. The jeans went first, then his boxers, and then he was on the bed with her, naked, nothing between them.

Just like they'd been before, but there was a different meaning now. This wasn't just heat and passion. That was there, but there was also a sense that this was forever. This was their promise. This was a partnership of two people who were always going to work together to be the best they could for each other.

And to help the world as well.

She loved that he would be able to heal people the way he had her. And she loved that there was a tough side to him as well, one he was coming to accept and control.

He was a powerful being with heavy burdens, and she would be here by his side to watch him explore his gifts.

He lifted his head. "I wasn't trying to read your thoughts, but they were so sweet." He put a hand to her face, grazing her cheek. "But I'm going to help you, too. I'm going to take you to do everything you ever wanted, before you were injured. Anything in general. I'll have a job in this world, but it doesn't come before you. Because you're the only reason I'm here."

She flushed, unable to believe she'd made such a difference for this beautiful man.

She wrapped her arms around his neck, pulling him close, looking down his long body at every delicious part. His wide chest, the little hairs running over tanned, gorgeous abs. His trim hips and muscular butt. The lines at each side of his hips that pointed down to the part of him she desperately wanted to feel inside her.

She wriggled against him, moist, ready, and he smiled and spread her legs farther, kneeling between them. With one smooth move, he was in, and she wrapped her legs around him to trap him.

Not that she needed to. She could tell by the tension in his body he was in just as much heaven as she was.

She held her breath and then let it out slowly as

her body adjusted to the searing heat inside her, so hard, so filling. Making every nerve in her light up like fire, ready to go. Then he started moving, his eyes closing in effort for a moment as he got them started.

And then things were smoother, more comfortable, as they found their rhythm together, but no less heated. No less passionate.

His fiery blue eyes met hers and held, and she felt how beautiful she was reflected in his gaze.

She'd never expected to be loved like this, but now that she had it, she'd never let go.

As pressure built inside her, raising her higher and higher, she tucked her head in against him, holding on tight, ready to fall. When she tipped over the precipice into intense, resounding pleasure, he went with her, uttering her name as he held her tight, jerking within her, setting off more sensation inside her as he tensed and went even harder.

"Luc," she uttered like an oath as she finally finished, feeling completely sated, her body radiating pleasure. Like she'd been soaked in it.

He grinned and leaned over her, putting them

nose to nose as he rested on his forearms. "Yes, love?"

She wrapped her arms around him and kissed him hard, sliding her tongue in to mesh with his, enjoying still having him inside her, at least for a few more seconds. "I love you. I really do."

He nuzzled her nose. "I love you, too."

Then he rolled out of her and curled up alongside her, hiding her in his arms, nuzzling the back of her neck. She could feel his huge body behind her and drew the sheets around them both.

Then she turned over so she could snuggle facing him, both of them on their sides.

"So," she said, "tell me all about dragons."

He grinned and happily obliged.

EPILOGUE

A couple weeks later, Luc and Hallie were visiting Erin and Zach, talking about how the house hunt was going and enjoying lunch.

Luc had brought Bastien over to see what he thought about Bo, but right now, the cats were currently hiding under separate pieces of furniture, trying to decide what they thought about one another.

When they heard a knock on the door, they all looked up warily.

Ever since the oracle had said she was sending a new dragon, they'd all been waiting with bated breath.

Zach squared his shoulders, taking a deep breath as he walked over the sparkling granite entryway to open the door. He took one last look over his shoulder at the rest of them and then swung it open.

Standing on the step, hands in pockets, looking as relaxed as you please, was Redmond Corinthian, the ruby dragon.

Dark-red hair, a rich, nearly purplish color that shimmered in the sun. Piercing green eyes in a catlike almond shape. Smooth skin. Tilted nose. High cheekbones.

A tall, muscular body. As per usual for the most sexual dragon on the planet, Ruby looked good.

Even Luc could admit it.

Zach, however, was less than pleased. He drew in a deep breath, then took a step back, then slammed the door shut in Red's face.

Then he strode back to the rest of them, shaking his head. "I'm going to call the oracle right now. I'm telling her Sapphire was one thing. I'm *not* taking Ruby. He's not staying in my house, with my mate."

"I won't seduce her!" called a pleasant voice from the porch.

"Who was that?" Erin asked, eyes wide.

"Oh my gosh, he was beautiful," Hallie said.

Luc narrowed his eyes, and she flushed. "I mean, not as beautiful as you. I meant more objectively. Like a piece of art." When Luc still didn't look mollified, she pulled him close. "Oh, come here, you. You know you're the only one I want."

They snuggled, and Zach paced, letting out a sigh. "I'm going to send him right out on the street where he belongs."

Erin put a hand on Zach's. "Hey, come on. You're a leader, like it or not, and you're supposed to help the other dragons get used to this world."

Zach muttered something unintelligible, but then his mate rose on her toes and kissed his cheek, stroking a hand through his hair, and he melted. "Fine. I'll help him at least find a place to get settled. But that deviant isn't staying anywhere within ten feet of you. Hear me?"

She giggled and nodded, looking over at Hallie. "So jealous."

Hallie gazed up at Luc. "Wouldn't have it any other way."

"Onyx! Sapphire! Come out and let me meet your wenches! We can share!"

Zach's face went pale, and he rolled up his sleeves, surely heading for the door to lay out a beatdown. Luc laughed as he grabbed the other man by the jacket, pulling him back.

"Calm down," he said.

"You heard him," Zach said.

"He isn't from here," Luc said. "We'll teach him the rules."

"Like that'll do any good. That guy is wacko."

Luc looked at the door. He didn't know Red well. He knew some of his powers, and he knew he was renowned for his beauty and sexual prowess. He'd always thought those were odd dragon powers, but if the oracle sent him, that meant she thought there was something he could do for this world.

"Good point," Zach said, hearing his thoughts and answering reluctantly. He inhaled and let out a deep breath and then stormed to the door, opening it and blocking it with his huge body.

Luc stayed back with Hallie, while Erin moved

forward to take a peek.

"No, you're not coming in yet," Zach's voice boomed. "Not until we get some things straight. No. Shut up a minute." Red said something unintelligible, and Zach moved forward, shutting the door behind them so they couldn't hear much of what was said.

They did hear Zach yell something about their mates not being "wenches" just as the door slammed shut.

"That's going to be interesting," Hallie said, looking at the door.

"Yeah," Erin said. "Zach might want you two to stay if there's going to be another dragon."

"I guess we can see how that goes," Luc said. "I don't know Red well. But after everything you did for me and Hallie, we're happy to help however we can."

Erin gave him a grateful smile. Then her eyes darted to the door. "I'm going to go spy from a side window. Want to come?"

He shook his head, putting an arm around Hallie's waist as Erin ran off.

"You don't want to go?" Hallie asked, looking up

at him.

He sat in one of the large chairs in the entryway and pulled her onto his lap. "I'm fine right here. Whatever comes, we'll handle it."

She snuggled into him, and he smiled as he thought about all the adventures that were coming. The other dragons. The fights against evil. All of it sounded exciting.

A new world, a new him, a new love.

With Hallie by his side, everything was possible.

* * *

* * *

I hope you enjoyed Sapphire Dragon and Luc and Hallie's story! Thanks for reading and please leave a review if you enjoyed it!

ABOUT THE AUTHOR

Terry Bolryder is the author of over twenty bestselling shifter romances. She grew up surrounded by mountains in the western part of the United states and loves the great outdoors. In her spare time, she enjoys reading and snuggling with her husband (who she likes to think would make a wonderful bear shifter). She writes about big, handsome men with larger than life hearts and protective streaks a mile wide and the amazing, curvy women that come to be their mates.

Made in the USA
Monee, IL
22 June 2022